SHOVEL READY

SHOVEL READY

A Novel

ADAM STERNBERGH

CROWN PUBLISHERS

New York

Copyright © 2014 by Adam Sternbergh
All rights reserved.
Published in the United States by Crown Publishers, an imprint of the
Crown Publishing Group, a division of Random House LLC, a Penguin
Random House Company, New York.
www.crownpublishing.com

CROWN and the Crown colophon are registered trademarks of Random
House LLC.

Library of Congress Cataloging-in-Publication Data
Sternbergh, Adam.
Shovel ready / Adam Sternbergh. — First edition.
1. Assassins—Fiction. 2. Suspense fiction. 3. Dystopias. I. Title.
PS3619.T47874S49 2014
813'.6—dc23
2013012901

ISBN 978-0-385-34899-7
eBook ISBN 978-0-385-34900-0

PRINTED IN THE UNITED STATES OF AMERICA

Jacket design by Will Staehle
Author photograph: Marvin Orellana

10 9 8 7 6 5 4 3 2 1

First Edition

To
Julia May Jonas

Every human being who has ever lived has died,

except the living.

—FREDERICK SEIDEL, *"The Bush Administration"*

1.

My name is Spademan. I'm a garbageman.

—this fucker.

I don't care.

Don't you want—

Just a name.

I have his address.

Great.

See this fucker—

I said don't.

Okay.

The less I know, etcetera.

How much?

What I said. To the account I mentioned.

And how will I—

You won't hear from me again.

But how do I—

The dead guy. That's how.

I don't want to know your reasons. If he owes you or he beat you or she swindled you or he got the promotion you wanted or you want to fuck his wife or she fucked your man or you bumped into each other on the subway and he didn't say sorry. I don't care. I'm not your Father Confessor.

Think of me more like a bullet.

Just point.

———

—best friends. At least that's what I thought. Then it turns out *she's* fucking *him*.

Please, ma'am. I will disconnect. And this number doesn't work twice.

Wait. Is this safe?

Which part?

Aren't they listening?

Of course.

So?

Doesn't matter.

Why not?

Picture America.

Okay.

Now picture all the phone calls in all the cities in America.

Okay.

Now picture all the people in all the world who are calling each other right now trying to plot ways to blow America up.

Okay.

So who the fuck do you think is going to care about you and your former best friend?

I see. Will you tell her—

No.

Will you tell her when you see her that it was me who sent you. It was me.

I'm not FedEx. I don't deliver messages. Understand?

Yes.

Good. Now the name. Just the name.

I kill men. I kill women because I don't discriminate. I don't kill children because that's a different kind of psycho.

I do it for money. Sometimes for other forms of payment. But always for the same reason. Because someone asked me to.

And that's it.

A reporter buddy once told me that in newspapers, when you leave out some important piece of information at the beginning of a story, they call it burying the lede.

So I just want to make sure I don't bury the lede.

Though it wouldn't be the first thing I've buried.

It might sound hard but it's all too easy now. This isn't the same city anymore. Half-asleep and half-emptied-out, especially this time of morning. Light up over the Hudson. The cobblestones. At least I have it mostly to myself.

These buildings used to be warehouses. Now they're castles. Tribeca, a made-up name for a made-up kingdom. Full of sleeping princes and princesses, holed up on the highest floors. Arms full of tubes. Heads full of who knows. And they're not about to come down here, not at this hour, on the streets, with the carcasses, with the last of the hoi polloi.

Yes, I know the word hoi polloi. Read it on a cereal box.

I never liked Manhattan, even back when everyone still liked it, when people still flocked from all over the world to visit and smile and snap photos. But I do like the look of Tribeca. Old industrial neighborhood, a remnant from when this city used to actually make things. So I come across the river in the early morning to walk around here before dawn. Last quiet moment before people wake up. Those who still bother waking up.

Used to be you'd see men with dogs. This was the hour for that. But there are no dogs anymore, of course, not in this city, and even if you had one, you'd never walk it, not in public, because it would be worth a million dollars and you'd be gutted once you got around the corner and out of sight of your trusty doorman and your own front door.

I did see a man once walking a million-dollar dog. On a treadmill, in a lobby, behind bullet-proof glass.

Feed-bag delivery boy on a scooter zips past me, up Franklin, tires bouncing over the cobblestones. Engine whines like he's driving a rider-mower, killing the morning quiet. Cooler on the scooter carries someone's liquid breakfast. Lunch and dinner too, in IV bags.

Now it's just nurses and doormen and feed-bag delivery boys out at this hour. Tireless members of the service economy.

Like me.

Phone rings.

—and how old is she?

Eighteen.

You sure about that?

Does it matter?

Yes. Quite a bit.

Well, she's eighteen.

Got a name?

Grace Chastity Harrow. But she goes by a new name now. Persephone. That's what her friends call her, so I hear. If she has any friends.

Where is she?

New York by now. I assume.

That's not much to go on.

She's a dirty slut junkie—

Calm down or I hang up.

So you're just a hunting dog? Is that it?

Something like that.

Just a bloodhound in a world of foxes?

Look, you need a therapist, that's a different number.

She's somewhere in New York, so far as I know. She ran away.

I have to ask. Any relation?

I thought this was no questions.

This matters.

To whom?

To me.

No, I meant any relation to whom?

T. K. Harrow. The evangelist.

Now why should that matter?

Famous people draw attention. It's a different business. Different rates.

As I said, I'll pay double. Half now, half later.

All now, and as I said, I need to know.

Yes. She betrayed his—

I don't care.

But you'll do it?

A fake name in a big city. Not exactly a treasure map. More like a mile of beach and a plastic shovel.

She said she was headed to New York. To the camps. They call her Persephone. That's a start, right?

I guess we'll find out.

May I ask you another question?

Go ahead.

You can kill a girl, just like that?

Yes I can.

Fascinating.

Before you transfer that money, you better make sure you ask yourself the same thing.

———

I hang up and write a single word on a scrap of paper.

Persephone.

Pocket it.

Then take the SIM card out of the phone, snap it, and drop the phone down a sewer grate, hidden beneath the cobblestone curb.

No motives, no details, no backstory. I don't know and I don't want to know. I have a number and if you've found it, I know you're serious. If you match my price, even more so. Once the money arrives, it starts. Then it ends.

Waste disposal. Like I said.

It's an old joke, but I like it.

Truth is, I never spend the money.

2.

I start at the camps. The biggest one's Central Park. At first the rich at the rim of the park hired private guards to chase them out, tear down their tents, send them scurrying, by any means necessary. Then there was a couple of incidents, a few headlines, then a skinning. Private guards got creative. Peeled a kid and hung him upside-down from a tree. That didn't play well, even in the *Post*.

All that's over now. The rich never come out to the park anymore, could give a shit about Strawberry Fields, the camps have been here three, four years, long past anyone caring.

Dozens of pup tents, like rows of overturned egg cartons. Dirty faces. Drum circles and dreadlocks.

I ask around.

The first person who knows her has a forehead full of fresh stitches.

Bitch cut my face.

Band of white peeks up over his waistband. Not boxers. Bandages.

Looks like she didn't stop there.

He picks at a stitch.

Hardy-har-har.

Kid nearby pipes up.

I knew her. Cute girl. Quiet. Pink knapsack. Wouldn't let anyone near it.

You know what was in it?

Drugs, be my guess. That's what most people hold on to tightly around here.

He's a skinny kid with a shaved head, sprawled out on a ratty towel. Sleeveless t-shirt and sweatpants and thousand-dollar sneakers, barely smudged. The kind of kid who's used to having other people run his errands for him.

I ask him the last time he left the park.

Me? Why? Truce with the cops seems cherry enough.

You have everything you need right here?

More like I don't have anything I don't need, you feel me?

Pretty girl peeks her head out of his tent before he shoos her back inside. Then he shoots me a look like, What can you do? Duty calls. I ignore it.

How well did you know her?

Persephone? Not as well as I would have liked. Common theme among the dudes living here, by the way.

You make a move?

Ask my friend with the stitches how that would have worked out.

So where did she go?

Just left in the night, far as I know. I woke up and all her stuff was gone. Most of my stuff too.

Any clue where she was headed?

No. But if you find her, tell her I want my blanket and my stash of beef jerky back.

You mind if I talk to your friend in the tent?

Smiles. Shrugs.

She's all yours.

Pretty girl. Young. Far from home. Overalls and a red bandana tied over hair she cut herself. Seems sisterly. Figure she's more the type Persephone might have opened up to.

I tap on the tent, then we walk out of earshot.

—we weren't close. Talked a few times. Then I heard she left.

Why?

Made too many enemies. Or rather, unmade too many friends. Headed to Brooklyn, was what I heard. Maybe towards family.

That helps.

By the way, you're not the only one come asking around for her.

Do tell.

Southern guy. Buzz cut. Those mirrored glasses, what do you call them—

Aviators.

That's it.

How long ago?

Maybe a day. Maybe yesterday.

I say thanks. Then ask her a few things I shouldn't.

How long you been here?

Me? A year, give or take.

Where's home?

Here.

Before that?

Don't matter.

And how old are you?

Look, you can't fuck me, if that's what you're asking.

That's not what I'm asking.

Well, maybe you can. Don't give up too easy.

Thanks for your time.

Viva la revolución.

So it turns out my Persephone has a reputation. Everyone knows someone who knows someone who knows. The people who got too close to her usually have some memento. Something permanent, in the process of healing.

3

Like I said, I don't like Manhattan.

Like Brooklyn even less.

Personal reasons.

But I don't like Brooklyn.

Never been to Staten Island. The Bronx only on business.

Queens I could take or leave.

But then, I'm from Jersey. Wrong side of the river. So maybe my aversion is hereditary.

Though to tell the truth, aversion and hereditary are both words my father never would have used. Might have cuffed me if he heard them coming out of my mouth.

He was a garbageman. A real one. The kind with garbage.

Didn't like pretension.

Didn't like the word pretension.

But he loved Jersey. That much he gave me.

I even tried to live in Brooklyn once, believe it or not. Didn't take. But I tried it. Thanks to my wife.

I had a wife.

Believe it or not.

And I was a garbageman too, if you're interested, a real one. The kind with garbage, like my dad. Left that too. Left most everything eventually.

Whatever hadn't already been taken away.

Now I kill people.

The end.

———

People get upset when you say you kill people.

Fair enough.

But wait.

What if I told you I only kill serial killers?

It's not true, but what if I told you that?

Now what if I told you I only kill child molesters? Or rapists? Or people who really deserve it?

Wavering yet?

Okay, now what if I told you I only kill people who talk loudly in movie theaters? Or block the escalator? Or cut you off in traffic?

Don't answer. Think it over.

Not so self-righteous now.

I'm just kidding.

There's no such thing as movie theaters anymore.

Subway, wheezing, barely makes it over the bridge, though I swear I feel that way every time.

The problem in this city used to be too many people. Now it's not enough. And when only poor people use something, no one takes care of it. Roads, schools, neighborhoods. Subways too.

Rusted-out, empty, watch the track-slats pass as we travel. Moaning drunk curled in a corner, already done for the day. Pissed his pants, and not recently either.

Now to Brooklyn, that victim of tides.

My father took me to the beach once, pointed toward the water, eighty yards out. I thought, No way that ocean ever gets back to here. Two hours later, it was lapping at our ankles. And I thought, stupidly, No way it ever goes back out to there.

Money comes, the people come. Money goes, the people recede. After the blackouts they left, then after the boom they came back, then after the attacks they left again. Not everyone, of course. Just the people who'd tried to turn Brooklyn into the suburbs, got a whiff of a dirty bomb, figured fuck it, and moved to the regular suburbs.

Anyway, tide's out now.

Brownstones are back to being barren. Concrete blocks where windowpanes went. Concrete blocks are the blind man's stained glass, someone once told me.

After the attacks, the second ones, the whole borough emptied out. A boom, bust, and bang economy. The squatters and lesser vagrants just moved right back in. Like they were returning from a long vacation.

The Brooklyn camps in Prospect Park are more scattered, less crowded, less refugee pile-up, more Cub Scout jamboree. Tambourines and Hacky Sacks. Come nuclear winter, Hacky Sacks will prevail. A lone sack, being hackyed, on some burnt-out horizon. We'll know civilization, and jam bands, survived.

I ask around. Same stories. She moved through here, quickly. I could have guessed. Not long for camps. She seems to attract the unwanted element in the open air.

Luckily the next step isn't too hard to figure. Supposedly she's headed toward family. And it turns out that her father, T. K. Harrow, the most famous evangelist in America, has a famous financier brother living in Brooklyn.

Yes, I know the word financier. Just don't ask me to say it out loud.

In my business, the disadvantage of the famous is that they draw more attention. The advantage is that you can find out almost anything you need to know in about fifteen minutes, either online, from public records, or through a few well-placed calls. Because you know who has a good idea of who lives where?

Garbagemen.

They notice. Know addresses. Not everyone. But the notable ones.

So I make a few well-placed calls.

Find out a certain Lyman Harrow lives in a mansion in Brooklyn Heights. Likes to throw things out. Expensive things.

Keepsakes.

People remember.

Which is why I keep a few well-paid contacts who are still in the garbage business. They're not nosy.

I just tell them I work on missing persons.

Don't tell them how the persons end up missing.

I don't care at all, and even I find this house beautiful. Brownstone, limestone, some kind of moneystone. Real stained glass, the kind for people with eyes. And four armed guards, making their hardware visible.

I wait and watch from across the street.

I used to ride this route, back when I lived in Brooklyn, back before Times Square, so I can remember when neighborhoods like these were basically sponges to soak up all the excess cash sloshing over from across the river. All these grand old brownstones, bought up and gutted. Scaffolding like skeletons. Blue tarps like funeral shrouds. Crews of Mexicans tearing out the drywall. Armed with hammers. Wearing dust masks. Eating lunch on the stoops, dusted white.

Haunting these houses like ghosts.

No one ever wanted to keep the insides of these old houses. Just the facades. That's what they always said about brownstones.

Good bones.

So it was out with the old, in with the expensive-and-new-designed-to-look-like-it's-old. Gut renovations. The insides torn out and tossed in a dumpster out front.

I know, because I used to pick up all the trash.

But then disaster struck and Brooklyn got seedy. Now gangs of men with masks and hammers might still visit your brownstone, but they're not coming to renovate your kitchen.

Still, a few stubborn holdouts hang on. Wall Street types like Lyman Harrow, who can't stomach the thought of ever running from anything. Everyone leaves, Lyman Harrow hires security. Everyone scurries, Lyman Harrow hunkers down. Lyman Harrow, his butler, and his four armed guards. And he assumes his money should function like a moat.

Which, in his defense, most of the time, it does.

Wall Street types. Funny to call them that.

Given there's no such thing as Wall Street anymore either.

A nurse comes. She's an unusually pretty nurse.

Rings the bell. Butler answers. Honest-to-God butler in white tails and everything.

Disappears behind a heavy door.

This seems straightforward enough.

I ring. Same butler.

I'm here to see Mr Harrow.

Regarding?

It's about his niece.

Follow me.

The butler leads me inside and up a curved staircase. The whole place is wood, highly polished, like it's all been carved out from the trunk of one giant dead tree.

At the top of the stairs, the butler motions for me to stop. I glimpse that same pretty nurse disappearing through a different doorway down the hall. Her hands held high. Elbows at an angle. Like she's prepping for something sterile.

Butler's short but solid. Brazilian maybe. Built for more than polishing silver. Not a linebacker but definitely the kind of guy who, if you ever find yourself in a cage with him, he's the one who winds up walking out.

Holds up a white-gloved hand. Asks politely.

Arms out please.

He gives me a quick once-over with a metal-detector wand. Traces my outstretched arms. Brushes my coat pockets.

Wand squeals.

He reaches a white-gloved hand gingerly into my coat pocket and pulls out a metal Zippo lighter. Flicks it open, fires it, then snaps it shut and places it on a silver tray on a table by the door.

Swipes again. Down each inseam. Over my boots.

Wand squeals.

I shrug.

Steel-toe.

He seems satisfied. In any case, he's mostly just putting on a show. He wants to let me know that, in this house, he's the last line of defense, and he's got more skills on his résumé than just answering the door.

Stows the wand back in its stand.

Turns a gold knob the size of a softball.

And in we go.

———

Lyman Harrow turns from his windows, which look out over Manhattan.

You have a view like this, you don't give it up. Am I right?

The furniture is mahogany. The smell is old library. The carpets are the expensive kind. With patterns.

He opens his arms. He offers drinks. I decline.

Well, what can I offer you then?

Your niece. Grace Chastity.

You're too late. She's already gone. My brother sent you, I assume.

That's a fair assumption.

It's the only reason I let you in. Apologies for the security. But you know. The rabble. City is thick with them.

Not a problem.

Harrow's half-hidden behind a huge desk, which is bare, save for a bottle, half-emptied. He pours himself another cognac, his glass as big as a fish bowl. Overall he has the unkempt air of the weird rich. Gray hair past his collar, slicked back with something greasy. Sweatpants and a crisp tuxedo shirt, untucked and open at the throat. Can't tell if he's halfway to getting dressed or just all the way to no longer caring. Then again, it's a classic tapper uniform. Perfect attire for the beds. And sure enough, he's got a luxury model tucked away in the corner. Which also explains the nurse I saw.

He sips.

Do you know why my brother sent you?

I hoped you'd tell me.

Well, he's plenty mad at his daughter, I know that. Mad enough to send her running to me. And to send you after her. And so on. I assume you've met Mr Pilot.

Not yet.

Okay. You will. In any case, Grace rang my bell. Came from those dirty encampments. But I haven't even spoken to T. K.

in ten, eleven years. And I haven't seen Grace since she was a toddler.

Swirls his cognac, which looks expensive even from across the room. Sniffs it.

Glances up at me.

She's not a toddler now, I can tell you that.

I take it you and T. K. aren't close.

No. Especially once I made it clear to him I had no interest in the family business.

Which is?

Heaven, of course. At least ten generations of holy men. Harrows were converting seasick sailors on the *Mayflower*. Then savages in the new world. Then anyone who'd listen. It was a bull market. We Harrows sell heaven, that's our business.

Another sip.

Or, at least, we sell tickets.

But not you.

My brother and I both grew up to be carnival barkers in the end. We just wound up working in different carnivals. If I'm going to wail and pray and fall to my knees, I prefer to do it at the stock exchange.

And what about your niece?

What about her?

Did you help her?

Oh. No. I'm afraid not.

Why not?

I am among the, I don't know, five hundred richest men in America. And T. K. is at least twice as rich as I am, and commands an obedient army besides. If he'll do this to get to her, send you and whoever else might follow, what do you think he'd do to me if I tried to keep her from his clutches?

More cognac.

I don't need that trouble. Not for a little girl. My only goal was to get her off my hands as quickly as possible. My hands and my conscience.

So then what.

She spent the night. I owed her that much. She's family after all. Then this morning I introduced her to a couple of men. I found them on the Internet.

What kind of men?

Not the nice kind, I'm afraid. Man with a van, that sort of thing. There were two men, actually. And they did come with a van, as advertised. I think they make it their business to find jobs for little girls.

You know where they went?

I didn't ask.

What about the van?

Hard to say. It was black. Or blue. Black or blue.

Drains his drink.

No offense, but I don't generally take to interrogations by my brother's hired helpers. Not Mr Pilot. Surely to God not that maniac Simon. And while you seem perfectly pleasant, Mr—

Spademan.

Mr Spademan, I can honestly say I don't think I'd like to see you again.

Understood. Thanks for your time.

And thank you for stopping by. Say hi to Mr Pilot for me, when you do meet him. He can't be too far behind you. As for me, if you'll excuse me, I'm going to return to my bed.

His unit sits in the corner of the study, tucked away, like a treadmill, though one that obviously gets a lot of use. It, too, looks out over Manhattan. It's titanium, part coffin, part luge sled.

Yes, I watch luge. The only winter sport worth watching. That and skeleton, which is like headfirst luge for nihilists.

I put on my coat.

With this view, I wouldn't think you'd need that. The bed I mean.

Well, then you don't really understand the bed.

He undoes his cuff links, lays them on the desktop. Rolls up his sleeves, gets ready to slip in. Steps out from behind the mahogany desk. Wearing shower slippers. Crazy tycoon toenails, untended. Grown out like talons. Head of a financier. Feet of a gargoyle.

Notices me noticing.

Thomas will show you out. Thanks for coming by, Mr—

Spademan. Like I said.

Of course.

The butler walks me out of the study discreetly, leaves me in the hall, then returns to help Lyman Harrow tap in.

That sure is a top-of-the-line bed.

Yes sir. Thank you for coming by. Good day.

We stand on the moneystone stoop.

Look, if there's anything you remember about those men who came—

I really should be getting back inside.

—any marks or details.

The butler considers. Looks like he could use a nudge.

Think about this. Mr Harrow's brother sent me to do the same thing those men are going to do, except I'll be a lot quicker. With nothing extracurricular.

The butler looks away. Considers. Then holds up one white glove.

Points to the back of his hand.

One of the men. He had a tattoo. Right here.

Do you remember what it looked like?

Like a fishhook. Except twisted. Into the shape of an eight.

I pull a marker and a scrap of paper from my pocket.

Can you draw it?

The butler waves off the paper, uncaps the marker, and sketches it on the back of his own white glove. Holds the glove up again.

Sure enough, like he said. A fishhook, twisted into the shape of an eight.

&.

An ampersand.

He caps the marker and hands it back to me. Then peels off the white glove and hands me that too. Pulls a fresh white replacement from his pocket.

Don't worry. Mr Harrow gives me plenty of gloves. Likes me to keep my hands as clean as possible.

I would imagine.

I pocket the drawing.

Thank you.

He nods and digs a pack of cigarettes from a breast pocket. I wait while he lights one for himself. Then I point to the pack.

You mind?

He frowns. Then knocks one loose for me. I stick it in my mouth. Smile thanks.

Then curse.

Goddamn it.

Patting pockets.

I forgot my lighter.

Turn my best hangdog to the butler.

Family heirloom. Gift from my grandfather. You mind?

Mr Harrow will not want to be disturbed.

Finger to my pursed lips.

Quiet as a church mouse. Scout's honor.

The butler's already started on his cigarette. Considers chucking it. Takes a long drag instead. Nods toward the door.

A thanks-buddy backslap as I head back inside.

Crush the unlit cigarette in my jacket pocket.

Never smoked and I'm not about to start.

Must be the choirboy in me.

Don't get me wrong. I went to Sunday school for about ten minutes as a kid. Didn't take. Not the important stuff, anyway.

The core beliefs. Right, wrong, etcetera.

As you might have guessed.

The Zippo's still sitting on the dainty silver tray. I snatch it up though it's not like I need it. I have a dozen more just like it in a box back home.

Buy them in bulk.

Turn the gold knob quietly.

In Lyman Harrow's defense, it's true that money often functions like a moat.

But not today.

Harrow is already swaddled and gone in the bed. Sedatives, feed-bag, sensors connected. IV tubes in all the IV holes. That nurse really knows what she's doing.

The bed truly is top-of-the-line. Polished touch screens. Metallic surface I can see my face in.

Harrow dozing lightly.

I lean in.

He's lost in the dream, eyes fluttering under closed lids. I check to make sure he's under, which is more than he deserves.

I keep a box-cutter stashed in my steel-toe boot, by the way. It's enough to set off a metal detector, but then, so is the boot. Not my fault if you don't double-check.

Pull the box-cutter out, extend it, place it against Harrow's throat, and pull across, pressing deeply. Hold his forehead down. It works well enough.

Watch him bleed out on the leather. Blood puddles on the touch screens.

Stained glass.

4

They'll find him but they won't know who did it. Someone named Spademan.

Spademan's not my real name, by the way.

Got it from a garbage can.

I head straight up to Montague Street with the white glove in my pocket and look for the first Internet kiosk I can find.

Since the beds got up and running, sucking up all the bandwidth, the boring old Internet survives mostly as an afterthought, kept alive like a public utility for people who can't afford to tap in. So, like a decaying neighborhood, all the money in the Internet moved out. And, like a decaying neighborhood, the Internet is now mostly a refuge for poor folks and perverts, people in the shadows, by choice or not. Just a place where you can log on to advertise your junk, then swap it for someone else's junk, then revel for a day in new junk.

Or a place where you can find a man with a van to take away your problem little girl.

Yes, there are pockets. Niches. Chat rooms where like-minded rebellious citizens can scrawl graffiti. Plot upheaval. Organize something like the camps.

But for the most part, it's just a digital cesspool. Free market, at its freest.

I take the first kiosk I find on Montague, though it's not

really right to call it a kiosk. It's just a screen on a pole, with a metal keyboard sticking out, and a stool on an angle like a cactus arm.

I take a seat, tap a key, and swipe a paycard to get started. Not my paycard, of course. Belongs to a car salesman, name of Sidney, who lives out in Canarsie. Or, rather, lived. Apparently, Sidney rubbed someone the wrong way. Who knows. Maybe sold them a lemon.

In any case, paycard works fine.

I log on and run a search for AMPERSAND+TATTOO. Get back a bunch of photos, but nothing promising. College lit majors, mostly, showing off frosh-week mistakes.

So I run a search instead for AMPERSAND+BROOKLYN. Same deal. One listing for a local bar for bookish types, long since closed.

Behind me, coming down Henry Street, I hear sirens, which is unwelcome. Twin cop cars doppler past in a hurry, lights whirling, whoop-whooping like a war party, heading south.

I guess the butler.finally found Mr Harrow.

I pull out the glove the butler gave me.

Examine his shaky sketch.

&.

Think again about what he told me.

A fishhook. Twisted into the shape of an eight.

I run a search for AMPERSAND+EIGHT+TATTOO. Still nothing.

Then just AMPERSAND+EIGHT. Find a jazz combo in Queens.

Then AMPERSAND+FISHHOOK.

Actually, ISHHOOK.

F key doesn't work.

Fucking kiosks.

So I type in AMPERSAND+HOOK instead.

Bingo.

It's a missed connection, of the type that litter the Internet. Cute-girl-I-saw-you-reading-on-the-subway kind of thing.

This one says: You, burly type with a fondness for whiskey. Me: cat's eye-glasses, matching you drink for drink. Not sure, but I swear we had a moment at night's end out in the street waiting for a car service, in the light of the neon ampersand. If I was right, meet me tonight back at the Bait & Switch in Red Hook. You bring the bait. I'll bring the switch.

Run a search on the Bait & Switch, which turns out to be a titty bar down in Red Hook, with a knock-three-times, private-members S&M room in back. Switches, riding crops, cat-o'-nine-tails, bullwhips. Whatever your pleasure, they've got a cabinet, and it's very well stocked.

And also, possibly, an outreach program. Job placements for wayward teenage girls.

Service jobs.

Maybe my tattooed henchman is an extremely loyal employee. Who recruits reluctant women. Ungently.

Long shot, I know, but I write the address down anyway, then log off.

Ball up the butler's stained white glove.

Drop it down the sewer.

Same place I'm headed, more or less.

5.

It's well past dark by the time I start walking down the water-front. Not the safest walk at this hour, and the shortest route on foot would be straight down Columbia Street. But I still can't bring myself to walk down Columbia Street.

Personal reasons.

So I take the scenic route, winding through Cobble Hill and Carroll Gardens, past the blocks of boarded-up and blacked-out brownstones. Occasional bonfire burns in a bay window. Nearly all the trees on these picturesque streets long since chopped down for salvage or firewood.

Stump-lined streets.

If only my Stella could see this. What's come of our old stomping grounds.

My Stella.

She was my wife.

That's not her real name either. Just a nickname that stuck. At least between us.

I skip our old block. Give it a wide berth.

Like I said, I like Brooklyn least of all.

And then I finally reach the raised Brooklyn-Queens Expressway, cross under, and head into what's left of Red Hook.

All the wiring's waterlogged, corroded and useless, so there's not a streetlamp lit in any direction. Streets are dark and the warehouses derelict, windows all broken by bored kids with good aim. In the road, oily water waits in puddles, camped out by the overstuffed sewers. There's a dead-dog smell and, sure enough, a dead dog, chained to a fence to guard an empty lot, then left on its leash to starve and fester.

Flies feasting.

Red Hook's version of a welcome mat.

Red Hook sits low on the water, and from some parts you can see the Statue of Liberty, and supposedly the whole place used to feel like a frontier town, a refuge to escape to when the rest of Brooklyn got flooded with money. But then Red Hook got flooded with water. A few times. Waist-deep sewage and six-foot-high watermarks staining the walls. Storm of the century came three times in a decade, so this neighborhood was in trouble even before Times Square. After Times Square, forget it. Anyone with a car and a suitcase headed for higher ground.

Some people still live here. The poor with no options, packed into public housing. Hardy stubborn squatter types who don't mind living in an abandoned row house that's made up mostly of mold. Business interests that rely on an element of privacy. Since the floods, the whole neighborhood stinks like the underside of a wharf. And, like the underside of a wharf, this allows a certain kind of life to thrive.

My plan is to drop in at the Bait & Switch, knock back a few drinks, and ask some questions. Maybe I'll even get lucky. Unearth my Persephone.

Instead I'm only halfway down Van Brunt Street when I stumble on the same pair of police cars I saw back in Brooklyn Heights, with an ambulance besides, all pulled over at the end of Coffey Street, parked by the Valentino Pier.

Roof-lights swirling. Turning the dead-end block into a disco.

On the stoops, wallflowers watch.

Guess the cops weren't headed to Harrow's after all. Though I'm not too eager to wander over, in case they're out on some Lyman Harrow–related APB. Then I hear a crackled command on one cop's walkie-talkie and realize that's not what they're here for.

Two cops shine their Maglites into the back of an abandoned van.

Black van. Or blue. Black or blue. Too dark to tell.

Even so, my chest clenches.

Which is weird.

Because what exactly am I worried about?

That someone got to her first?

Still, no one should go this way. Not like this.

I shoulder closer through the sparse crowd of mostly bored onlookers. One cop halfheartedly tries to shoo us all back while also checking texts on his phone.

Phone chirps. Incoming message. Cop smirks. Funny text.

I edge to the front of the crowd.

Van's back doors are flung wide open. Blankets piled up inside.

Body under the blankets, if my eyes see right. Or bodies.

My eyes see right.

EMS guys yank the first stiff from the back.

Not a girl, though.

A man.

Dump him on to a gurney.

Arm flops over the side.

Back of his hand. A tattoo.

&.

So much for leads.

———

First body lays splayed out on the stretcher, bloody and neglected, and it's not like TV. No one solemnly says a prayer or pulls a sheet up over his head. These EMS guys have other things to worry about, like rolling up another gurney and pulling the second body from the van.

Also a man. Also mangled.

Signs of serious knife-work.

I ask the texting cop what happened. He doesn't even look up from his phone.

Who knows? Lovers' spat? Some random psycho? Ask me, smells like some homo 69 gone very wrong.

I wince. Play squeamish.

Looks like those guys got slashed to ribbons.

Cop shrugs.

Sometimes passions run high.

Any leads?

Cop looks up finally.

Human garbage lives around here? Take your pick. I'm just surprised whoever did this didn't torch the van. Would have saved us a trip. Let fire worry about it.

How long's that van been here?

No more than a few hours, maybe. Only got called in because some thugs pried the back open, looking to loot it, and got spooked. Found more than they expected and phoned 911. Not until they'd stolen both stiffs' wallets, of course. And stripped out the stereo.

Phone chirps again. New text. Cop smirks again.

I say thanks as I retreat back into the crowd.

Don't really worry about him remembering my face.

I'm not that memorable.

Just a garbageman.

———

I should have remembered.

Bitch cut my face.

First rule of the runaway. Always carry a blade.

And don't be bashful about using it.

She definitely wasn't bashful.

Which is when I wonder if maybe I've been underestimating this Persephone.

My Persephone.

Interesting girl.

And still has some claw in her yet.

6.

The Bait & Switch is hard to miss, since it's the last place in Red Hook, housed in a small brick building at the end of Van Brunt Street, on the last block before you walk straight into the river. And turns out the butler was more right than he knew. The bar's sign has a bright neon fishhook, twisted to look like an ampersand, between the words BAIT and SWITCH.

Spot it six blocks away. Bar must be running a private generator to get that much wattage out here.

Ampersand blazing like a flare sent up over an otherwise pitch-black street.

So if Persephone came this way looking for help, this is the place she would have ended up.

Assuming she didn't know that this is where those men were planning to take her in the first place.

Or that she came this way.

Or that she needed help.

I figure Sherlock and the other cops back there will probably just call it a night. Didn't seem too concerned with cracking the Case of the Man with the Ampersand Tattoo.

Couple of lowlifes in a van. Not exactly top priority. And no one wants to hang out in Red Hook after dark.

Then again, one of the cops might remember that tattoo, spot this neon sign, and decide to earn a paycheck for once and maybe poke around.

If so, I'd like a head start.

Door of the Bait & Switch jingles as I head inside.

Sparse weeknight crowd. A few dedicated lonelies parked at the bar. One couple fighting at a round-top in the corner, hissing at each other in inside voices. Her: cat's-eye glasses. Him: at least six whiskeys down. Looks like they made their missed connection after all.

I claim a stool.

Bartender wanders over. No ampersand tattoos. Just anchors on his forearms. Like Popeye.

What can I get you?

I'm looking for a girl.

He smiles.

Aren't we all?

She would have come in a few hours ago. Might have looked scared. Or maybe not.

He unsmiles. Puts a shot glass down in front of me.

Sorry, but I'm not paid to notice anything here except empty glasses.

Fills the shot glass up with whatever's on hand. Something amber and alcoholic. Screws the cap back on. Anchors flexing.

But if you're looking for company, we do have a back room. Plenty of girls back there. Some of them scared-looking. If that's what you're into.

I toast him with the shot glass.

No thanks. I'm good.

Well, why don't I leave you to your drink then? This one's on the house. Next one you can get somewhere else.

Then he trundles off to tend to the other drunks, like a gardener pruning a row of wilted plants.

———

As for me, I'm more or less back at the beginning. New York is big and my Persephone could be anywhere.

Needle in a haystack and that's not even her real name.

So I vow to look in all the usual places, starting with the bottom of this here glass.

I raise the glass. Solemnly promise. I will get to the bottom of this.

Down it.

I know it's a cliché to be a hard drinker in my profession. But it's the one part I do really well.

Well, this, and that other part.

It's just all the stuff in between.

Camps have dried up. Uncle's dead, thanks to me. And she just left two bodies in a van. Quick and fearless with a blade, I'll give her that. Technique's rough, but certainly no shortage of guts. Then again, it's not too hard to take down two men if you've got a decent-sized knife and they don't.

Just start stabbing.

I motion for another round, then remember I'm on the bartender's blacklist.

So if I'm a girl, maybe covered in blood, definitely alone in the big city, where do I head next?

Tiffany's?

If there was still a Tiffany's.

I guess I could always peek into the bar's back room. Interview a few of the dominatrices.

Plural of dominatrix. That word I had to look up.

But I'm not really in the mood to interrogate regular people right now, let alone ones wearing full-leather masks.

With zippers for mouths.

I need to get out of Brooklyn.

But I sit a minute more and try to formulate a theory.

On the run from her father, presumably. Did something bad enough that he wants her found but he doesn't want her back.

If I can figure out what, that might give me a hint where she's headed.

Not that I'm interested in motives. Just whereabouts.

But my brain's an empty blackboard. There must be a school for this somewhere. I'll enroll in the morning.

I finish the dregs of my drink.

Pull my coat from the stool-back.

Needle in a haystack. Never did understand that expression. Fuck searching, just buy another needle—

Bells on the door jingle. Like it's Christmas.

Bartender calls out to a squat Hispanic, freshly entered.

Hey Luis. You fuck that girl or what?

There's some amount of dumb luck involved in this undertaking, especially if, like me, you are not a gifted, trail-of-bread-crumbs kind of guy.

Dumb luck.

You just have to accept it and hope it comes when you need it.

Sometimes in the form of a squat Hispanic.

Luis is a livery cabdriver. Livery cab being a fancy way of saying Crown Victoria in need of new shocks. Apparently they still run livery cabs across the bridges, what few souls still make that journey.

Bartender leers while he wipes out a beer stein.

That piece of chicken. Tell me you banged her, Luis.

Luis is quiet.

She had blood on her. On her clothes.

I perk up.

We retire to the corner.

Take the two-top vacated by cat's-eyes and the whiskey connoisseur. They left earlier. Not together. Another missed connection, I guess.

Two rounds later, Luis tells me he drove this girl all the way to Central Park. Young, maybe eighteen, maybe younger. Approached him while he was outside the bar, finishing a cigarette. He says it was dark and he swears he didn't notice all the blood on her until they were halfway up the FDR. Caught the shine of it in the rearview in the sweep of a streetlamp. At that point, figured it was safer to just keep driving. Left her at the park's edge. Told her the trip's on him.

Did she say where she was going? Back to the camps?

That theory doesn't sit right with me, but why not cross it off first.

Luis shakes his head.

No. Somewhere else. To Bethlehem.

To Bethlehem?

That's right. That's what she said. To Bethlehem.

Buy Luis another round. Settle up with old anchor arms.

That's not what she said. She said Bethesda. But close enough.

Luis is in no mood to take a second trip back into the city but he drops me off at the F and I settle in for a long slow journey on the rattling train.

The park is long since dark.

The angel of Bethesda watches over a barren fountain, the

water finally turned off years ago. One wing stolen, the other half-broken. Her face spray-painted red, as in shame.

A girl in a bundle at the base of the fountain.

I step in.

Hello Persephone.

She looks up. Hooded sweatshirt, frayed denim, Doc Martens. Blond curls matted. Hands balled in pockets. Face tear-damp. Voice steady.

I've had a long day, I have a knife, and I'm not looking for trouble.

Pocket moving. Like she's tightening a grip.

I step closer.

Mind on that blade.

I'm not here to hurt you.

Which is exactly the opposite of true.

7

Whatever's going to happen, it's not happening here.

I coax her up.

She stands. Jeans cut to mid-calf. Docs look like hand-me-downs. Technicolor laces. Like a dreamcoat.

Hands balled in hoodie pockets. Still got that knife somewhere.

Not sure how to make the introduction. Friend of your father doesn't seem like a promising opener. Friend of your uncle, even less so.

I work with an outreach program for kids.

God, I hardly half-believe this even as I say it.

You look like you could use a hot meal.

There is no part of her that trusts me. But every part of her wants that meal. Every part of her wins. She hoists up a knapsack that maybe used to be pink. Half a rainbow decal with a little pony, peeling.

Motions with her chin, hands still balled.

You lead.

I walk out the west side, her five paces behind me. The park is dark and dead and, on the streets, it's no different. Not a soul on the sidewalk and it's not even eleven. Doormen sit behind glass, watch us pass, shotguns propped on their laps like homesteaders. Cop cars sail by, sirens wailing, but we could shoot up a flare and they won't stop.

Most of the restaurants on Amsterdam shut down in the past few years, once the moneyed types stopped eating out. Now there's two shuttered businesses for every one still open, big gaps in a rotting smile. But there's still a coffee counter here and there, in among the army surplus stores. Posters hawking half-price gas masks and Geiger counters, with a voucher for a free donut next door.

I know a place, the American Century, popular with nurses. The lively clatter of steerage. The servant class, between shifts.

We take a booth.

Where you from?

South.

How long you been here?

A few weeks. I came for the camps.

How'd that work out?

Not so good.

So what's next?

I don't know. I'm not coming with you though.

Not an option. In any case. Though I do have a room.

Dirty fingers disembowel a white dinner roll. Stuff it in like it's medicine.

Looks like you could use a manicure at least.

Fuck you. You sleep three weeks in a park, see what it does to your cuticles.

Just an observation.

You're a beautician too?

I dabble.

Quick smile. Despite herself.

Then I'll take a mani-pedi both, if you're offering.

Well, that I can't promise. But I do have a clean bed. An extra bed, I mean.

Wait, don't you work for some kind of shelter? For wayward teens?

I thought you might be tired of sleeping in open spaces
with a bunch of people you don't know. I have a guest room at
my place. Door locks too.

And where are you?

Hoboken. I'm a Jersey boy. Like Sinatra.

On her second roll, eating quickly.

Who's Sinatra?

I don't usually do it this way, just so you know. I don't track
people down and then take them out to dinner. I prefer if it
works the same way on both ends of the job. The less interac-
tion, the better.

But whatever you think of me, which by now may not be
much, I'm not going to cut a woman open in Bethesda Fountain. Or a diner bathroom. I prefer when I find them dreaming in their beds.

And yes, I'm sorry to bring that up, but that is what I'm
here to do. It's a real conversation stopper, I know. You may
say, how can you do it? That's not a question I usually enter-
tain. But remember what I said.

I don't know these people.

I'm just a bullet.

Rolls, soup, cheeseburger, cake. Tears through it like she's
eating for two.

Two bills to the waitress.

We're about ready to head out.

. I want to ask her how old she is. Though I haven't had
much luck with that question today. Truth is, I realize there's
a small chance she's too young. Too hard to tell anymore.

Every fourteen-year-old a supermodel, every forty-year-old still trying to pass for a teen. My Little Pony backpacks used to be a reliable indicator. Same with heels and belly piercings. No more.

Maybe the voice on the phone lied. And if she's not eighteen, that means I take her home, set her up with a hot shower, maybe bus fare, let her sleep eight hours for the first time in weeks.

If she is eighteen, same thing, except no shower or bus fare, and she'll sleep a lot longer than that.

Waitress brings my change.

It's silly, I know. This fixation on birthdays. But tell that to a kid with a learner's permit. Or a kid signing up for the draft.

And as much as I'm starting to maybe hope it's not the case, if she is eighteen, she's an adult. And deserves to be treated as such.

So I spill it.

How old are you anyway?

Why? Are we going to vote?

Hostel regulations. Overnight guests. Children-adults. You can stay either way. It's just for bookkeeping purposes. Head counts. That kind of thing.

She shifts in the booth. Like she's wondering which way to play this.

Swipes back a dirty curl.

Proudly age of majority. Just had my eighteenth a few weeks back. That's partly why I headed to New York.

Happy birthday.

Figured it was time to blow out my candles, New York—style.

Greatest city on Earth. Once upon a time.

She squirms a little in the booth.

I think I might take you up on that extra room after all. If the offer's still open.

Of course.

I watch her dirty face. I'll let her have the hot shower, at least.

And the door locks, you said?

Of course.

Well, then so should we get going?

You're not lying to me are you?

She smiles. A glimmer of trust.

No, I'm not. I'm eighteen. Freshly minted grown-up.

I leave a fat tip on the tabletop. Some kind of penance, I guess.

She shifts again, restless.

Damn, I just can't get comfortable. And it's so hot in here. Are you hot?

She slides out of the booth. I sit still.

She stands. Empties out her hoodie pockets. Lays an underfed coin purse on the table, looking skinny. Next to that, a five-inch bowie knife in a stained leather sheath.

Parting gift from my father. Don't worry. I know how to use it. But I won't.

I sit still.

Girl alone in the big city. You understand.

She slips the knife in her boot. Unzips her hoodie. Flaps it back like a cape.

God, that's better. Sorry, I get these flashes.

Hands on hips. Leans back.

Baby bump.

8.

The way it happened was, it started as business software. Some kind of fancy teleconferencing gimmick. Clunky helmets, silly goggles, but once you plug in, it was pretty amazing. 3D around a table. Avatars that look surprisingly like you. Pick a tie, any color. Your choice. Dreams really do come true.

That was maybe ten years back.

And if we've learned anything in this once-proud world, it's that once someone figures out how to do something as miraculous as that, it's only a matter of time before someone else soups it up so you can use it to suck a horse's cock. In pretend land.

Or run a brothel. Or be a holy Roman emperor.

In pretend land.

Soon people were running around, half-centaur, or space-alien furry, or Kareem Abdul-Jabbar, or what have you. Fucking Chewbacca.

Literally fucking Chewbacca.

Then they got rid of the helmets and goggles and made the whole thing about a thousand times more convincing and all you had to do was get in a bed. But beds are expensive. From basic model to deluxe silver bullet. The basic ones are just tricked-out cots, but the top end are like shiny half-coffins, personal escape pods, with a bunch of touch screens to guide you into the dream, sensors to put you under. Full immersive experience.

As real as real.

That's the pitch.

As for the specs, I can't tell you. I'm not an IT type. And I've only been in a bed a few times.

Not the deluxe kind either.

Anyway, they figure out that this is clearly where the money is. But the bandwidth required is huge. So they build another network, call it the limnosphere, everything shifts, and they leave the boring old Internet for the rest of us. Internet goes to seed, of course, but the rich don't care, because the rich are now lost in the limnosphere. It's like the Internet but better, much better, because it's an Internet you can live inside. Or the rich can. The costs are astronomical, of course, but then again, that's why they call them the rich.

After that, the math is pretty easy. Thirteen hours in first class from New York to Tokyo, or slip into a bed and hold your meeting in minutes, with you at the head of the board table, glowing like a gladiator pumped up on steroids and Cialis. Drop twenty thousand on diminishing returns at the plastic surgeon, mending the same old curtains, or spend it on a month-pass to the limnosphere, sashaying down Park Avenue like Marilyn Monroe's prettier sister. With a leopard's tail.

In pretend land.

Still, it was just part of life for the first while. An addictive, maddening, seductive, destructive part of life, but part of life. They called it limning, or tapping in, or going off-body, or whatever, and most people dipped in and out. For the first while.

But after the second attacks and the dirty bomb? Then the rich just up and disappeared. White flight, except they didn't go anywhere. They just drew the curtains and retired to their beds full-time. Hire a nurse to check your vitals, sign up for the weekly feed-bags, station armed guards to watch the gates, and goodnight moon. Goodnight stars. Goodnight world.

That was maybe five years ago.

My point being, usually how this works is I get a name, find an address, let myself in quietly, and introduce myself politely to an old man's atrophied body in a coffin that's already half-assembled. Even if the old man is only thirty. Feed-bags will keep you alive, but they won't help you keep your youthful glow. Or your hair. When you start limning full-time and go on permanent bed-rest, you pretty much leave your body behind.

So you lie there, half-mummified and lightly drooling. And unfortunately for you, someone back here in the nuts-and-bolts world has decided they can't let that grudge slide after all. And they found my number. And I found you.

Quick slit with the box-cutter and it's all over.

Except maybe not. Not in the dream.

There is a theory, unprovable I guess, that when you die, there's a last little burst of neural activity. The brain's last helpless, hopeless little sigh. Normally, this would be your blown kiss to a cruel world as you exit, stage left.

Yes, I did a play in high school. Mitch in *Streetcar,* if you must know. Would have made a better Stanley.

But if you're in the limnosphere, in the dream, at that last moment, this little burst of brain activity loops. Your final seconds skip forever like a record. Even after they unplug the mummy and cart it to the furnaces. You remain as a data burp, hiccupping, some tiny line of code still in the dream.

And you don't know this. That's the theory. You're just stuck in that last moment, an eternal *right fucking now,* endlessly repeating for however long the batteries of this planet hold their juice.

No one knows if it's true, of course, because how would you test it? They say they have programmers combing the code for these little hiccups, but most of their resources are on other things. Like developing newer, better, more tactilely realistic horse cocks.

But it's true enough that some people try to game it. After awhile they're not happy enough with just the dream. They pick a program, their ultimate fantasy. Movie star. Fuck your neighbor. Crowd roar when you take the podium on Inauguration Day. Or sight the podium in your rifle-scope. I don't know. That one fantasy you can never say out loud to anyone. The one moment you would happily live in forever.

They time it out to the second. Hire someone to stand by. Lean in. Make sure the lids are fluttering. Clock hits zero. Put you down.

Sounds weird, I know. But then again, people used to hang themselves while jerking off.

Funny thing is, most people choose real-life memories. Your husband turns around in the airport, back from the war, and it's really him. Your miracle mother comes out of her coma. You cut class and the bedroom door swings open and your high-school crush finally drops her dress. What people want is to live in that heart-swell of *I can't believe this is happening,* over and over again.

Black-market agencies sell this service. Split-second timing. Our watchers are the industry's best. Results guaranteed.

If they fail, who's going to tattle? You're lost in a loop somewhere, your needle bobbing on the inner edge of the record, at the far shore of a vast ocean of black.

So you better hope they loop the right moment.

Because if they miss, that person standing over you,

watching you fall into the dream, if they miss, even by a moment, half a moment, or just a breath, then you're stuck, and
your husband never turns around and you never know if he
made it, or your mother stays sunk in her coma with you an-
chored bedside worrying, or you stare at that bedroom door
forever, knob trembling, wondering what's about to come in.

I choose not to believe it. Seems too convenient, and besides,
if I buy that, then I might believe I'm not ending someone.
I'm just pausing them, maybe in the happiest moment they've
ever had.

That seems cheap. It's a cop-out. So I think of it the
other way.

Most of them have already given up on this world, the
nuts-and-bolts world. This party's over and they've moved on
to the after-party. They've left their bodies behind.

I'm just sweeping up.

In any case, that is what I am used to. All jobs don't go like
that, obviously. But you'd be surprised how much overlap
there is between people with the money and desire to disappear into pretend extravagance forever, and people who want
those people dead.

What I am not used to is eighteen-year-old runaways carrying bowie knives and babies.

But that's fine.

Because she's pregnant.

So our business here is done.

I kill men. I kill women because I don't discriminate. I don't
kill children because that's a different kind of psycho.

And while I'll admit I've never tested this particular scenario in practice, I think it's safe to say that pregnant teenagers fall under the category of a different kind of psycho.

Harrow I can handle. Sometimes circumstances change. My policy in this regard is actually pretty simple. I give back the money. What you do then is your business. As for me and the girl?

Our paths uncross.

In the meantime, though, what I can do is offer her that hot shower after all. And a bed. And bus fare. And maybe waffles for breakfast.

Back here in the nuts-and-bolts world, we can't all be holy Roman emperors. But we do enjoy a waffle now and then.

Like I said, I live in Hoboken. Jersey boy. Like Sinatra. I wasn't making that up.

And I did play Mitch. Would have made a better Stanley. Hated learning lines though. Hated crowds. Hated acting, basically. Enjoyed kissing the girl who played Stella though. One day as a stand-in.

And my dad was a garbageman. An actual garbageman, I mean. So after high school I followed him into that line of work.

And I married the girl who played Stella.

My Stella.

Better than any encore.

PATH trains to Jersey shut down years ago, half the underground tunnels collapsed. No one commutes from Jersey to Manhattan anymore.

So I own a boat.

Just a rowboat with an outboard. Lock it up with a heavy

chain at a west-side pier. I give Persephone a handkerchief to tie over her mouth like an outlaw. I do likewise. This time of year, you don't want to be drinking the Hudson. Not even spray.

Any time of year, for that matter.

Then I yank the cord and we cross state lines.

Behind us:

American Century, with a CLOSED sign. Which is weird, because it's 24 hours.

Counterman sighs, expecting a hold-up, knows the protocols, starts scooping out bills from the tray.

Southern gentleman asks in a Southern accent about a young pregnant girl, possibly with a man.

Counterman shrugs.

Waitress is more helpful.

I seen them.

That's what a big tip gets you these days.

Heard something about Hoboken. Sinatra. Girl didn't even know who he was.

Says it in a tone of what's this world coming to, am I right?

Southern gentleman nods.

Much obliged.

She smiles back.

Smile distended in the convex of the aviators. Clownish.

Also distended: Her blood, her brains, on the back wall, like a thrown pie.

Turns the long revolver on the counterman. Like a diviner's rod, seeking water.

Finds blood.

9.

The apartment is palatial, just because everyone cleared out. After Times Square, finance types were the first to evacuate. Packed up their pinstripes and skedaddled. For them, Times Square was like a roach bomb, sent them scurrying, either to full-time bed-rest or safer cities or both. Most even left the furniture behind.

Their hasty exit, my real-estate opportunity. For a few months there, after Times Square, when no one thought anyone would stay, you change the locks on a place, it's basically yours. Mayor declared a tenant amnesty, a homesteader's free-for-all. Disputes got settled with fistfights, not leases, and the cops were otherwise occupied. It settled down eventually. Turned out there was plenty to go around.

Come reelection time, the mayor clamped down. Ran on a platform of rebuilding and rebirth. Stood on a dais and declared the city shovel ready. I think he was right, but not in the way he meant.

I probably could have moved to Park Avenue if I'd wanted to, but it felt like the right time to retreat across the river. Always preferred this side, in any case. Even if it means you need to own a boat.

And there's no more Wall Street, not in New York. There's still the actual street, in the city, that you can walk on, but that financial part? Moved elsewhere. London, Beijing, Seoul. For awhile, they tried swapping stocks in the limnosphere, set up a virtual exchange, but there were too many distractions, too much money to be made indulging other vices. So they set up a separate network and do all that money-swapping somewhere overseas. All the bankers and brokers relocated. Good riddance. And thanks for the divan.

Okay, divan is a word I had to look up. A visiting lady-friend said it to me once. Said she admired it.

My hand-me-down divan.

Persephone is admiring my divan. Stretched out, leaning back on it, more obviously pregnant. White wifebeater under the unzipped hoodie, revealing a sliver of belly. I'd guess maybe five months. Like I'm a doctor now.

I give the tour.

Room back there. Lock on the door, as promised. Bathroom's there. Clean towels etcetera. I sleep out here.

Thanks.

Hugs the guest pillow to her chest. Asks an obvious question.

Why are you being so nice to me?

It was a sad day when people started to ask that routinely, don't you think?

She laughs.

I don't really remember when they didn't.

You have a change of clothes?

She shakes her head. Unzips the rainbow knapsack with the decal of My Little Pony. I half-expect a tinier pony to come out.

Instead, a bottle and diaper inside.

You won't need those for awhile.

I know. I just like having them with me. Remind me why I'm doing this, you know?

Makes sense.

The knapsack was mine when I was a little girl. Always made me feel safe. I hope to pass it on, if she's a girl.

Looks a little worse for wear.

Yeah, well. I couldn't find the part of Central Park with the Laundromat.

She smiles.

You're not from some youth hostel, are you?

Me? No. I am from Hoboken though.

Are you going to hurt me?

No.

Were you going to hurt me?

This one's tougher. I say no. Because I would have tried to make it painless. Still a lie, I know.

Well, thank you. For your help. I haven't met too many people here who would help me.

Not a problem.

You listen to music?

No.

What do you listen to?

I hold up a hand. Moment of silence.

The city quiet.

I listen to that.

Lot of people tapped in here, huh?

Yeah. Not most. But a lot.

I guess I should be getting to bed.

Yell if you need something. I'm a light sleeper.

She looks me over. Then asks.

How old are you anyway? I told you. It's only fair.

Me? I'm you, plus fifteen years.

She winces. Laughs again.

God, I hope not.

———

Morning. Making waffles.

I mix batter, then head down to the street corner. Pick up takeout coffees, bagels, and the *Post*. Three comforts that outlived the apocalypse. *Daily News* went under and the *Times* long since disappeared into the limnosphere. Now it's just a ticker running through rich people's dreams.

But God bless the *Post*. They still publish. On paper.

I get back, she's up and dressed. Left her a sweatshirt, which on her grew into a dress.

Sorry about the fit. All my clothes are garbageman clothes.

It's clean. It's great.

You sleep okay?

Yeah. About three weeks' worth.

She giggles.

What?

You have a waffle iron.

Yes I do.

You don't really strike me as a waffle-iron kind of guy.

Best way I've found yet for making waffles.

Can't argue with that.

It was a gift. From my wife.

Eyebrow arches like a cornered cat.

Really. And where's she?

Deceased.

I'm sorry.

Cat relaxes. But slowly.

I slide a waffle on her plate.

So what's next?

I'm not sure. I've thought about Canada.

Last I heard, border's closed.

Yeah. I heard that too.

———

Plates cleared, coffee drained, waffles eaten.

Me doing dishes.

What can I say? I don't mind. I have a dishwasher too. Never used.

I like to clean up my own mess, as a rule.

She wanders over to the fridge while I'm not paying attention.

Stainless steel. Sub-Zero. A remnant from the Wall Street types.

You got any ice cream?

She glances over.

So sue me. I'm pregnant.

Opens the freezer.

Inside, a single Ziploc baggie. Inside the Ziploc, a butcher-paper-wrapped package, about the size of a brick.

Cat arches again, but playful.

What's this? Your secret stash?

I step over right-quick.

That? No.

She pulls the baggie out. Holds it up. Laughing now. Teasing.

What, you deal coke? Is that how you afford this place?

I snatch the bag back.

No. I do a bit of butchering.

Really?

It's a hobby.

Cool. So what's that? Please tell me it's bacon.

No. Not bacon. Just bones. For stock.

Well, look at you, Mr Julia Child. Let me know if you rustle up some bacon. I'm not a big meat eater but I've had weird cravings of late.

Rubs her belly.

I stash the bag. Close the freezer. Step between her and it.

Try to smile.

Can't let the cold out.

I don't have many visitors. So I get sloppy. Forget.

A freezer is a very bad place to keep your souvenirs.

10

Lazy Sunday. Me in an armchair. Her on the sofa with Sports.

Regular Cleavers.

I flip through the *Post*.

A22. Tiny item.

DEATH DINER DOUBLE SLAY.

The American Century.

I fold the paper back. Read it. Fill in the parts between the lines.

Surveillance tape caught him: Buzz cut. Aviators. Left the cash in the cash drawer.

Odd detail. Before he left, everyone dead, he holstered the pistol.

Stopped at the sink.

Washed his hands.

Buzz cut. Aviators.

Fondness for firearms.

This must be Mr Pilot.

Retracing our steps.

Bus-fare option doesn't seem like an option anymore.

I fold the paper up, slide it under the chair.

You know, you could stay here again tonight. A few more nights. I've got plenty of sweatshirts.

She yawns. Stretches out on the leather. Leather squeaks.

I just might.

Turns her head. Freshly showered hair.

Might even learn how to sleep with the door unlocked. If you're lucky.

Well, you're welcome to. Stay, I mean.

I gotta ask you again. Why are you being so nice to me?

Everyone's got to be nice to someone, right?

I get up. Pretend I'm tidying the kitchen. Try to plot plan B.

She turns back to Sports. Then stops. Sits up.

Stares me down.

My father sent you. Didn't he?

I stand like a dummy. With a dishcloth.

Who?

You know who. T. K. Harrow. Man of God.

I'm not religious.

Don't fuck with me. He sent you. It's the only way this makes sense.

I'm no good at lying. Same as acting.

Yes. He sent me. To find you.

(Technically true.)

And do what with me?

Keep you safe.

(Less true. Much less true.)

Bring me back?

Something like that.

She sits up straight. Picks up the bowie knife in its sheath from the coffee table.

Turns it in her fingers.

Well, let me tell you about how things work in my family, just so you know what kind of people you're working for. I stopped in on my uncle. In Brooklyn. For help? You know what he did for me?

(More acting. I hate this.)

No.

Set me up on a blind date. A double date. With two rapists. Or white slavers. Sex-trade assholes. Who the fuck knows?

Sounds like a charmer.

Lucky for me, the only place they didn't want to stick their grubby hands was in my boot.

She pulls the blade from the stained sheath.

Last I saw them, they were bleeding in a van in Red Hook.

I affect a shrug. Hapless Mitch all over again.

Sounds like they got better than they deserve.

She inspects the blade.

Does come in handy.

Sheaths it.

As for my father. The great T. K. Harrow? Leader of men? Pastor of sheep? Instrument of God?

Pulls the blade out again.

You've probably seen him on TV, right?

Don't watch TV.

That's okay. He's got bigger plans than that. Do you know what you've gotten yourself into? Do you have any idea what kind of man my father is?

I'm starting to get some idea.

No. I don't think you do.

Sheaths the blade.

But if you're on his payroll, you should know.

Puts the sheath down.

He's my father.

Pulls her knees up. Hugs them hard.

Yes. I know. I know he's your father.

No. You heard me wrong.

Hugs them harder. Arms round her knees. Arms round her baby.

I said, he's the father. He's the father. That's what I said.

11

I worked as a garbageman for ten years, more or less. Lost my father, my union card, and my marbles, in roughly that order.

Father went first. Died of a heart attack he worked a lifetime to earn. Strict regimen of smoking, bacon, and television. Man loved his Jets. Claimed they were Jersey's team. Forty-five millionaires in green helmets somewhere, carrying his heart into battle every week.

He didn't die on the job, thank God, stink of other people's garbage in his nose, not that he would have cared. When people asked his line of work, he never faltered. It was a good union wage and he wanted the same for me. My first day, he took me out to the truck yard, pulled the gloves on, drew a deep breath.

Smell that? That's security, son.

He was felled too young, in his own backyard. The plot of ground he'd bought by hauling other people's trash.

Barely room enough to fall down.

My mother sat on his chest, pumping, wailing, waiting for an ambulance that came ten minutes too late. Two streets with the same name. One avenue, one lane.

They picked wrong.

My mother tried. She was a nurse. Not the kind that fix feed tubes to rich people either.

By then I'd married my Stella. A Jersey girl, she swore never to live in Jersey by choice. I said Queens. She said Manhattan.

We split the difference and ended up in Brooklyn. Carroll Gardens. South, down by the expressway. The part that's not so gardeny.

My parents wanted to see a family. We were trying, but we weren't in a rush. We tried long enough to worry something might be wrong, but then we decided to stop worrying. We were young. My Stella wanted to be an actress. She rode the train to Times Square every day. Acting class in a shabby studio. Half my union wage.

I rode a route up through brownstone Brooklyn. Nicer neighborhood than we could afford. Nicer garbage too.

Boys on my truck gave us a nickname for a joke. Not garbagemen.

Trash valets.

It's hokey but it's true. You learn things hauling trash.

Lesson one. Don't buy cheap bags. They always tear. If not in your hands, then in mine. No discount bag ever went to its grave without being loudly cursed along the way.

Lesson two. There is nothing, and no one, that you will become attached to in this life that you will not one day discard.

Or they discard you.

Or you die.

Those are the only three outcomes.

A bartender I know once quoted me a poem, by a guy named Idol or something similar.

Every human being who's ever lived has died, except the living.

Lesson three.

You'll leave a trail of trash on this Earth that will far exceed anything of worth you leave behind. For every ounce of heirloom, you leave a ton of landfill.

That's not a poet. That's me.

What can I say? Sometimes you're on the toilet and you've already read all the magazines. Inspiration hits.

But that's the lesson. Your real legacy will be buried in a dump somewhere.

And the richer you are, the more trash you leave behind.

After the first attacks, the ones on 9/11, so they tell me, they took the rubble of the towers to a landfill.

Fresh Kills.

Sifted through it, searching for bodies. Bits of bodies. Bits of bits. Did their best and found what they could and left the rest of it there, buried.

True story.

Landfill became a graveyard.

The landfill doesn't care.

Never more than a whisper of difference between them to begin with.

Every garbageman has funny stories of stuff he's found on the job, of course. False teeth, brand-new flatscreen still in the box, a fake leg, a stuffed ferret. A double-ended dildo switches on, leaps out of the bag, twisting like an electric eel. Stuff like that.

People don't know what to do with something, they toss it in the trash. Brush off their hands. Expect it to disappear. Like magic.

Every garbageman has a funny story like that.

Here's mine.

We ran a route that looped past the crane yards by Columbia Street. Not six blocks from Long Island Hospital. We were done for the day and doubling back.

I was on the rear, riding shotgun. Like I'm security on a Wells Fargo stagecoach.

We roll past three bags, dropped in a vacant lot. Look like dim-sum dumplings sitting there. Illegally dumped. People miss their day so they hump their trash down the block. Can't stand the stink in the kitchen. Commonplace. These jokers couldn't even be bothered to drag the bags to the dumpster, maybe twenty yards away. Property of a private disposal company.

Company name stenciled on the dumpster.

SPADEMAN.

Bags in the dumpster are not our problem.

These three bags. Our problem.

Technically our shift's done. Plus no one's watching.

Still, I slap the side of the truck twice.

Driver stops.

Figure, our job is to keep the city looking nice. I'm a new neighbor here.

Let's make it look nice.

Pick one bag up, swing it overhead like a hammer toss. For a laugh.

Fling it in.

Second bag, swing it sidearm like David's slingshot, sighting Goliath.

Bullseye.

Third bag.

Lift the bag.

Funny heft.

Lower it. Slowly.

Though the God's honest truth is that I never would have opened it if I hadn't heard the gurgle.

————

They must have chickened out. Thought the plastic bag would finish it.

Cheap bags.

Always tear.

I carried a box-cutter to slash problem trash. Unbroken boxes, tangled twine. Shit like that.

Popped the blade up. Sliced the bag as carefully as I could. Like surgery.

Peeled the bag back.

Baby still breathing, barely.

That's my funny story.

First and last time I ever held a baby in my arms.

Not six blocks from Long Island Hospital.

They could have left the baby on the front door, rung the bell, run.

Instead, vacant lot became a landfill. Became a graveyard. So they hoped.

Six blocks.

So I took the trip they couldn't be bothered to take.

In some other version of the story, I adopted the baby. Named it. Raised it with my wife as our own. Told it the story, when it was old enough, of Baby Moses, left in the bulrushes, the one I learned in church as a kid.

This isn't that story.

I left the baby at the hospital. With a nurse. Answered a few questions. Signed a few forms. Went home to my wife.

Didn't check back. Didn't want to know.

And didn't tell my Stella until she read about it the next day in the *Post*.

———

Saw another item in the *Post* a few days later.

BAG BABY BURIAL.

Buried deep inside the paper.

Not even front-page news.

They needed a scandal. Baby left in a garbage bag? Story like that demands a villain. Someone to wear the black hat.

No one knew who left it. So that left me.

Post said I found it. Dumped it at the ER.

Didn't do enough.

Didn't even stick around to see if it would be okay.

I took a six-month leave. Union mandated. Half pay.

Weekly psychiatric consultations.

Daily visits to the bar.

Nightly nightmares.

Then the mayor finally busted the union. I tore up my card and cancelled my next visit to the shrink.

And I went back to work.

Someone's got to pay for all those acting lessons.

Even my Stella didn't understand. Not really.

She let it be. But I could tell.

Guys on the job too. Even the guys on my truck. Guys who were there.

Figured at the very least you stay. Cheer that baby back to life.

Maybe they're right.

Truth is, I wasn't going to sit in a waiting room so a nurse could tell me that the baby I just found in a garbage bag died.

I peeled that bag open so carefully it was like I was delivering my own baby.

So scared of what I would find inside.

I couldn't do that twice. Wait for news. Wait to know.

Sit there. Hunched over. Waiting.

Clutching my garbageman gloves.

In the waiting room.

With all the other expectant dads.

12.

Pass me not O gentle Savior,
Hear my humble cry.
Whilst on others thou art calling,
Do not pass me by.

Street-corner church service. Soap box preacher. Big crowd.
More popular in these end times.

Persephone's news put me back on my heels.
I don't like to be back on my heels.
First response, usually, is extend my box-cutter, find
someone to apply it to.
But that will not help in this situation. Much.
What I need is information. So I call my newspaper buddy.
Rockwell.
The one who says I'm always burying the lede.

I leave Persephone at the apartment, tell her don't open the
door for anyone, no matter what.
Then I meet Rockwell at a bar on Washington. Main ar-
tery in the proud heart of Hoboken. This bar opens early on
Sunday. Most do. It's not crowded inside, but it's not empty
either. A different kind of communion.
Bartender's the owner. My poet-quoting friend, Sebastian, from the Dominican. Named for the saint. So he says.

Sets us up with two shots.

Rockwell used to work for the *Times,* then he got fired. Turns out he has a lying problem, at work and in life. He once told me he's a descendant of the great American painter. Luckily I don't care much either way.

Now he publishes his own paper. *The Rockwell Report.* Conspiracies and cover-ups. He's the sole reporter. You can pick it up on any street corner. Literally. From a big pile. He leaves them there. For free.

Also runs a website, of course, on the old-fashioned Internet. But he likes the feel of paper, the stink of ink, so he says. Salvaged two copy machines from a bombed-out Staples near Times Square. Ran the Geiger counter over them. Only clicked a little bit, he claims.

Plus he wears horn-rims. So at least he looks like a reporter.

Tell me about T. K. Harrow.

What do you want to know that you don't already know?

Just empty the file.

Okay. Well, he runs that big church down South that sounds like a country singer. Hope Baptist. Hallelujah Hall. Something like that. Wait. Crystal Corral. That's it. So there's that.

What else?

The TV. That's where it all started. And it's lucrative.

That many people still watch TV?

Sure. You should get out of the city more often, you'd be surprised how many rabbit ears you still see. Not everyone's ready to jam an IV tube in their arm every time they want to escape, you know? Plus TV's basically free—at least, besides the money you send to your favorite evangelist in a little white envelope every week. Which adds up.

I guess so.

As for political clout, Harrow runs a weekly Washington prayer breakfast that's attended by, like, twelve senators and forty members of the House. So there's that. He more or less got our current president elected, first genuine fire-and-brimstone Bible-thumper in the White House. So there's that. And then he's got this new thing. Paved With Gold.

This is good. This is useful. This is enough to buy Rockwell another round.

Sebastian sets them down.

Paved With Gold. What's that?

It's this limnosphere thing. Signs up converts. Promises them heaven right now, here on Earth. Why wait, that's the pitch. Gold mansions. Endless happiness. Harp-playing-fucking-angels. All that stuff. Paved With Gold. You know, like the streets of Glory.

I thought the road to hell was paved with gold.

No. That's good intentions.

But how do people afford it? A bed alone is a fortune. Not to mention monthly tap-in fees, feed-bags—

Harrow subsidizes. He's got a camp somewhere down South. Rows and rows of beds. So they say. Limited space, so he can only accept the elect. How he chooses, God only knows. It's his earthly mission, he claims. Reason God put him here. Deliver his people from the torments of this bodily world.

Rockwell empties shot two. For him, two shots is just the stretching before the marathon.

So how big is his ministry?

How big? The biggest. When you can convince half the US government to get up at dawn to listen to you tell them what fucked-up sinners they are, that's pretty big. I don't know much about this fake heaven of his, but he's already amassed enough gold here on Earth to pave plenty of streets. Plus the political pull. He's got the president's ear. All that stuff. The only ripples on his pond I ever heard about are his kids. He has trouble with his daughters. So I hear. The oldest one supposedly went AWOL. Can't remember her name. Grace something.

Chastity.

Rockwell gives me a look.

Now why in the world would you know that?

Lucky guess. Figure it's got to be one of those virtues. You know. Constance. Charity.

Funny. Those are his other daughters.

So why'd she run?

Who knows with kids these days? Broke her curfew? Daddy wouldn't let her go to prom? Probably got knocked up by her boyfriend and decided to find some sugar daddy, try out the trailer life for a little while. No doubt she'll be back knocking at heaven's gates soon enough.

So where do I find him?

The South?

Seriously.

I think the main Paved With Gold camp is in a Carolina. North or South—can't remember which. Same with the Crystal Corral, the church you see on TV. But he's got satellite churches everywhere. There's even one in Times Square, or used to be. If you're looking to convert.

I just want to talk to him. About a job.

Well, if you'd like to meet the man in the flesh, you don't have to wait too long. He's headed here, to the city. I figured that's why you were asking.

What for?

Big crusade. Madison Square Garden. He's even paying to

get it cleaned up. Initiative with the mayor. You know, I hear the place is more lovely since the roof caved in. Supposedly you look up, you see stars.

And if it rains?

Fuck if I know. Tarps?

When is it? This crusade?

Dude, you've really got to get yourself a computer.

Downs his third.

I follow suit.

So this Harrow. Does he employ muscle?

Everyone employs muscle, Spademan.

You don't.

No. But I have you.

Rockwell pulls out a notepad. Starts riffling pages.

I do know of this one guy who works for Harrow. Supposedly a very scary dude.

I know the one you mean. Southern guy. Call him Pilot. Wears aviators. Big on hand-washing.

No, that's not him. This guy's black. Bearded. Name of Simon, I think.

Keeps riffling. Then stashes it.

Must be in my other notebook.

We're both on empty, so I signal Sebastian. Set us up again.

The dread pre-noon nightcap.

Bar's cleared out a bit. Brief lull between the first-thing-in-the-a.m. crowd and the afternoon-ennui rush.

Ennui. That's Rockwell's word.

Claims it's French.

Just two good buddies on the Lord's day, enjoying a Sabbath drink.

Bellied up to the bar.

Backs to the door.

Pilot walks in.

Picks wrong.

Broken horn-rims skid in the spatter.

Rockwell's forehead hits the bar. Exit wound swallows the shot glass.

I drop.

Sebastian grabs the sawed-off he stores by the Bushmills.

The shotgun speaks. *Barroom.*

I roll.

Sebastian martyred by bullets, not arrows, this time.

I scamper to the men's room to solemnly reconsider my predilection for box-cutters.

Predilection. Another Rockwell word.

Lock the door.

Men's room looks out over an alleyway.

Lucky.

By the time Pilot puts two new peepholes in the locked door with his revolver, I'm down the alley, cut right, right again, circle back to the bar's entrance.

Score one for the local boy.

Still.

Box-cutter.

I peek in the open door. Carefully.

Bar's dark.

Pilot comes back from the men's room.

Aviators look left. Right.

Reflect emptiness.

Walks back behind the bar.

Steps over broken bottles. Over Sebastian.

Stows his revolver in a shoulder holster.

Stops at the sink.

Washes his hands.

———

Half a block away, two patrolmen watch the action like Heckle and Jeckle on a wire.

Jersey's Finest.

Like most cops, like the whole of the NYPD, they're cash-strapped and half-privatized now, their salaries buoyed by moneyed interests with the city crying poor. So their main job is to stand watch and make sure the dreamers on the upper floors aren't disturbed. As for us carcasses down here, down in the grimy urban mosh pit, they don't much care what we do to each other.

I approach.

You've got shots fired at that bar on the corner.

We heard. Called it in. Waiting on backup.

I eye the pistol on one cop's belt. His hand instinctively hovers.

I reach in my pocket. Pull out my slush fund. Peel off a thousand cash. Then another.

Hoping I've guessed his caliber.

Mind if I rent your firearm? I'd like to make a citizen's arrest.

Cop looks at me. Looks at his partner.

I feed them their story.

There were ten of them. They overtook you.

Partner shrugs.

Seems fair to me. So long as you plan to split that.

I stride back through the bar's front door, unloading half the magazine as a herald.

Do serious damage to what's left of the liquor bottles behind the bar.

Seven shots echo. No one's shooting in here but me.

And Pilot's gone.

Fuck.

I fire off three more shots. Bottles fall like fainting ladies.

Run back to the apartment, cop's Glock in my waistband. We'll have to extend this to an all-day rental.

Yes, I have my own gun at home. Somewhere.

Thing about guns, in this line of work, they're not all that useful. Everyone has guns.

So they kind of cancel each other out.

Home. Secret knock. No answer.

Unlock the door. Shoulder it open. Slow.

Gun drawn.

Persephone on the sofa. Her back to me.

Huge headphones on her head like she's communicating with another planet.

Head bobbing. Eating ice cream.

She turns around.

Hey you.

Spoons another mound of Rocky Road in her mouth.

I went down to the corner. Hope you don't mind.

Licks the spoon.

What's with the pistolero, Sheriff?

I lock the door behind me. Scan the apartment.

We're alone, right?

Of course. What'd you think? I was going to throw a party?

I put the cop's gun in the drawer of a side table. Figure I can return it next time the department holds a toys-for-guns amnesty campaign.

In other words, I just bought myself a two-thousand-dollar teddy bear.

———

Pack your stuff.

What stuff?

Your bag. We have to go.

Oh my God, why? This is heaven. This is the most comfy place I have stayed in weeks. You have a shower! A glorious, hot-water—

We have to go. Now.

She holds up her hands, palms out.

Okay. Simmer down, Sarge.

She stuffs the headphones and balled-up laundry into her backpack. Zips up My Little Pony. Stands.

Still wearing my sweatshirt dress. And Docs.

I frown.

We need to get you some pants.

She slides the knife into her boot.

Don't worry about me. Let's go.

Doesn't ask why. Doesn't ask where.

So she trusts me.

Well that's good.

Not sure if it's smart. But it's good.

I need to stash her with someone I trust, which is a short list. Someone who can protect her, who has no love for the Church, and who I know beyond a shadow won't be tempted to creep up on her in the dark. That list is even shorter.

I do know one guy who qualifies. On all counts.

Mark Ray.

The only trouble with Mark is that he's tapped-out daily, a bed-rest junkie. So first you have to find him. Then you have to wake him up.

———

I'm paranoid about Pilot, so we skip my boat.

Hire a gypsy sloop to run us across the river.

Driver shouts over the outboard.

Destination?

Canal Street.

Canal Street? What for? Haven't you heard? Canal Street's dead.

I drop the conversation and we chop across the waves. Persephone hugs my arm, pressing tight against me. Then again, it's a small boat, I tell myself.

13

Canal Street. East side.

What used to be called Chinatown.

Once upon a time, you walked these blocks, you were wading waist deep in a river of people. The streets stank of spoiled seafood and the sidewalks were sticky with fish oil and ice-melt, dumped at day's end. And from sun-up to lights-out, these blocks would sing. Shouting, shuffling, haggling, hustling, vendors hawking knock-offs, shopkeepers harassing you in Cantonese as you pass like you stole something from them and they wanted it back. Fresh carp sunbathing on wood crates of packed ice. Hot dumpling soup for a dollar. Ducks, plucked and bashful, hung on hooks in a windowpane, like a warning to other outlaw ducks.

No more.

Chinatown met the same fate as the city, only more so. Last generation died off. Next generation moved to Jersey. Or upstate New York. Or the Carolinas. Or anywhere but here, downwind from a dirty bomb. Turns out no matter how deep your root system, you can always pull it up.

Have ducks, will travel.

So Chinatown withered. Went from egg-drop to pin-drop.

And the one last viable business in these parts moved indoors, out of sight, behind peepholes and passwords. And it caters to a clientele that is very, very quiet.

———

They call them dorms. Quasilegal tap-in flops, a hundred beds to a floor. Not the shiny kind either. Not like Lyman's. These are jury-rigged beds, not much more than cots and wires. It's strictly BYOFeedbag. Most people here don't care too much about food.

Mark's dorm of choice is a spot called Rick's Place. Run by a guy named Rick. The name's a *Casablanca* nod, mistranslated.

We head inside.

Rick is fortysomething, but he's smoked himself older. He's half-Chinese and skinny as a horsewhip. Wears silver skull rings on every finger and both thumbs. His black pompadour is coaxed to an impressively rigid sheen and he's got four facial tattoos. Chinese characters. Forehead, cheek, cheek, chin.

In answer to your next question, I've never asked.

He pulls on his cigarette. Cherry flares.

Mr Garbageman. I haven't seen you in a good long while. You decide to get back on the tap?

Hello Rick.

I tell you what. I'll give you two-for-one for you and your— girlfriend? Daughter? Sponsor? You know what? Forget I asked.

He gives Persephone a double-take.

I see congratulations are in order. Little litter of Spademen. Tell you what? Special today. Kids ride for free.

Persephone's perplexed.

How did you—

Hey, I'm Chinese. I can tell from the soles of your feet.

Rick's Asian lady-friend, Mina, comes stumbling out from a back room. She's a tool-head, like Rick, a technician, a gizmo, and likes to call herself Mina Machina. Long black hair and a thousand-yard stare because, unlike Rick, she's also a serious tapper.

We've never really gotten along.

She looks at me like she's about to say something, points at me, forgets, then half dozes off while she's busy forgetting. Spun around, she exits mumbling through a curtained doorway, stumbling off to look for something else she forgot to remember she forgot.

Rick shrugs.

What can I say? Soul mates.

Rick, I'm looking for Mark Ray.

He takes another drag. Looses a lanky ghost of smoke.

Sure, sure. Of course. Who isn't looking for Mark Ray? Our little angel. And I'm going to guess this is the very first place you looked.

The dorm is dark and drop-dead quiet. A former sweatshop, now a flop-shop, laid out like a battlefield hospital. Rows and rows of cots and a couple of tired-looking Chinese nurses, checking pulses.

A few muffled yelps escape from sleepers here and there. Hard to tell if they're cries of pleasure or fear. Or both. Two-part harmony.

Rick leans over.

You better let me do this. Mark is a heavy sleeper.

He winds through the cots. Spots Mark's crown of golden curls.

Persephone watches the room, wide-eyed.

I whisper.

I bet you've never seen anything like this back in Kansas.

I'm not from Kansas.

I know. But still.

I have. I have seen this before.

Still watching the room. Doesn't look at me.

This is what my father's camp looks like.

What?

Paved With Gold.

Then she says something else, in a croak. Half to herself. Like a joke.

In my father's house are many mansions.

I whisper.

What's that? Bible verse?

Nope. Sales pitch.

14.

Mark Ray used to be a youth pastor at a church in Minnesota. I met him a few years ago, after someone called me to offer me a job.

So how does this work?
  I just need a name.
  My name?
  No. I don't need to know your name. So long as you wire me the money. I just need the other person's name. The one on the receiving end.
  And that's it?
  That's it.
  Okay.
  So. The name?
  Mark Ray.

The caller's Minnesota accent hard to forget.

I tracked Mark Ray down to the Reading Room at the Public Library, the big one, in Bryant Park, with the stone lions out front.
  Not much reading in the Reading Room anymore. They tore out the shelves and put in server racks. Swapped the tables out, brought in beds. A high-end pit stop, a per-hour place, mostly targeting tourists, back when there were still tourists in New York.

Mark was walking among the beds, watching people dreaming. Angelic mess of curls on his head.

I walked up behind him. Figure I'd convince him that we should retire to someplace more private.

He turned.

So you've found me. That was fast.

Same Minnesota accent. Impossible to miss.

We sat on the front steps, watching the lions.

I don't do suicides.

Why not?

You want to kill yourself, kill your own damn self. That's between you and your god.

Yes, I guess it is.

He was sitting forward, elbows propped on his knees. Broad back. Young guy. Handsome as hell, if I can say so. Hard to see why he wouldn't want to live.

He held his hands flat together, like he was about to break out in prayer.

I understand why you have that rule. But my problem is, I can't do it myself.

Why not?

Mortal sin.

You Catholic?

No. Evangelical.

Then I don't think you have to worry.

He turned to me.

Are you a religious man?

No.

Never?

My parents dumped me at Sunday school a few times when I was young, keep me out of their hair. As for them, they tried to fight less on Sundays. Or at least keep their voices down. That was about the extent of it.

I see.

My father worshipped at the church of the New York Jets. Saint Namath and all that.

And you've never been tempted?

By religion?

Yes.

That's not the kind of temptation I have to worry about.

I was a pastor back in Minnesota. I used to teach a lesson on temptation. Or at least that's what I thought it was about.

So what's the lesson?

Do you know the story of Bathsheba?

Then it happened one evening that David arose from his bed and walked on the roof of the king's house. And from the roof he saw a woman bathing, and the woman was very beautiful to behold.

Mark filled me in. Back in Israel, in Bible times, Bathsheba was a woman who King David spied from his rooftop while she was bathing nude. He saw her and he was gripped with lust.

Gripped with lust. Not my words. Mark's. Or the Bible's. Or God's.

In any case.

Gripped with lust.

So David sent for her. He slept with her. And he impregnated her. Trouble is, Bathsheba was already married. To Uriah the Hittite. Who was not only one of David's trusted friends, but also a soldier in King David's army. But this didn't give David pause. It gave him an idea. Which he relayed to the army's commander.

Set Uriah in the forefront of the hottest battle, and retreat from him, that he may be struck down and die.

Mark paused the story.

So I've been teaching this passage a lot lately to my kids, my students. At first, I taught it the way that I learned it in Bible school. Not as a story of lust, or of corruption, but of temptation. You know, how God puts temptation in front of you. He allows you to feel your own weakness. To confront it. Just as Christ did here on Earth. Satan laid out the whole world to Christ, promised it to him, if only he'd bend a knee to Satan. And he felt it. Christ. He was tempted. But he didn't succumb. And we feel it too. Whether it's the apple in Eden. Or the desire to look back over your shoulder and watch Sodom crumble. Or spotting the most beautiful woman in Israel, bathing naked on a rooftop. I'm sure you have some secret temptation. Some secret shame.

I thought of a Ziploc baggie in a Sub-Zero freezer, while Mark waited for an answer that wasn't coming.

Okay. Well, your temptations are your own. I understand. My point is, I always thought that story was a lesson about temptation. This idea that the sin is not in the being tempted, but in giving in to the temptation. That is what God cannot abide. But I was wrong.

That's not the lesson?

No.

So what is it?

It's a story about wrath. It's not a parable at all.

No?

No. It's a warning.

———

Mark unpaused the story.

So on the battlefront, Uriah was slain by archers firing a rain of arrows down from a city's high walls. And the army's commander sends word back to the king, who he assumes will be crushed at this news. Right? But King David sends this message back to the commander.

Do not let this thing displease you, for the sword devours one as well as another.

I interject.

What were David and Bathsheba doing all this time?

They were busy fucking. Pardon my language.

Okay.

So King David's managed to pull off the perfect crime. No one suspects him, and even if they did, they'd say nothing. Because he's the king. He is blameless in the eyes of the world. If not in his own heart. Or in the eyes of God. And do you know what the last verse of that passage is?

No.

But the thing David had done displeased the Lord.

Well, yeah. You would imagine.

Mark pounded his palm like a pulpit.

But the thing. David had done. Displeased. The Lord. That is the lesson of the story. It's not about temptation. It's about vengeance. It's about wrath. It is about God looking down, and seeing what you've done, and being displeased.

Sure.

And do you know what happens when the Lord is displeased with you?

No.

You end up in New York, outside a library, begging some stranger to put you in the ground.

15

Mark. Persephone. Persephone. Mark.

The three of us back on the Chinatown street corner. Mark shies from the sun, still half in the dream. Dreamy.

He holds out a hand to Persephone.

Pleased to meet you.

Four letters tattooed across his knuckles.

DAMN.

When I first met Mark, farm-fresh from Minnesota, he was not the type to show up with new tattoos. Then again, he also wasn't the type to tap in for a week at a time. Had never been in a bed before he came to New York.

Still, I have to ask.

You didn't have these last time I saw you.

He flips his fingers, knuckles up.

What? These? Yeah. You like them?

He makes a fist. A letter on each finger.

DAMN.

Holds up his left hand. Makes a fist.

ABLE.

Holds the two fists together.

DAMNABLE.

I smile.

Very nice.

He turns his fists back toward his face, admiring them.

Right? I rented *Night of the Hunter*, got inspired. I've got a third one, too. Want to see?

That depends where it is.

He peels off his polo shirt. Still ripped despite the bed-rest.

Persephone perks up.

Mark turns his back to us. The third tattoo in block letters.

IRULE.

I tell him I don't get it.

He flexes his back. Shoulder blades spread like wings. The letters separate.

I RULE.

Nice. Very subtle.

He turns around.

It's more of a limn thing. If you ever tapped in, you'd understand.

Persephone chimes in.

Well, I like it.

Mark slides his shirt back on.

So should we head back to my place?

Persephone says she wants to grab a few supplies while we're here. Points to her legs. Still pants-less.

I peel off two bills. Feel like I'm her dad.

She smiles and disappears into a store.

Mark pulls his phone out and calls for a car, which seems to glide up before he's even pocketed the phone.

Mark calls shotgun. I hold the rear door for the lady and her shopping bags.

She arches an eyebrow.

So is this a blind date you've set up for me?

Not likely. You two look like brother and sister.

I know, right? Kinky. You could watch.

This stings. More than it should.

I tell her to watch her arm while I close the door, then lean in.

No offense, but you're not his type.

Why not?

He's celibate. By choice.

She smiles.

That's it? That's nothing. I know plenty of lapsed celibates.

That so?

You bet. Even lapsed a few myself.

We take the livery cab north toward Mark's apartment at the former Trump Tower off Columbus Circle. Not a Brooklyn livery cab either. This is no rusted-out Crown Victoria. It's a bulletproof limo, sleek as a sea lion.

Dashboard Geiger counter starts clicking and the driver steers a wide arc east to avoid Times Square. On these far-east avenues in Manhattan, heading uptown, you could almost believe the city is just like it was, only less so, cleared out, like how a sleepy summer Sunday used to feel. A few stray pedestrians. The random rogue yellow cab. Bright window signs promising blow-out sales.

But then we cut across midtown, which is a ghost town. Just trash and empty storefronts, long since looted. No more blow-out sales. Just blown out.

Dashboard Geiger chatters again and the driver cuts north.

The lack of tourists alone leaves it spooky. No one snapping photos, wrestling maps, gawking at skyscrapers, waddling along in a cluster, clogging the sidewalk, kids trailing behind licking soft-serve ice cream and wearing seven-pointed Statue of Liberty crowns made of sea-green foam.

Now there's plenty of room on the sidewalk for everyone, if anyone was out on the sidewalk.

No traffic.

Streets are clear.

The brighter side of car bombs, I guess.

They still go off from time to time. The car bombs. Planted by copycats with lesser ambitions. Easy to pull off now that no one's paying much attention to the streets.

Just another ongoing inconvenience of life in the big city.

As long as you're not standing too close, I find you flinch a little less every time.

In the end, half stayed, half left.

Simple math.

Not all who stayed hid in penthouses either. Some still run delis, wash dishes, fold laundry, mop lobbies, ride buses, drive cabs. They either moved back in to Manhattan when the last wave left or they still trundle in on broken trains from the outer boroughs. Too dumb or too poor or too hopeful to pull the plug and pack up and leave like the rest. All those diehards who refuse to let the city die.

In any case.

No mystery to it. Just basic subtraction.

Cut a city in half and you're left with half a city.

But you definitely notice the ones who are gone just as much as the ones who stayed.

The driver pulls up to the building, idles out front as we head inside.

Trump Tower. Former hotel and soaring glass eyesore. Named for the Donald of course. Long since dead. First thing the kids did when they pitched their camps in Central Park was lasso his statue, pull it down, put a dress on it. Last I saw it, it was still riding on the roof deck of a double-decker tourist bus, forever looping the park.

Mark's apartment's not the penthouse, but it's close enough. Not sure how Mark affords it. He's got some secret deal with some closet benefactor. He's coy about it and I don't press.

From his living room, we can see the camps in Central Park. Bonfires dotting the dusk.

On the avenues, police cars park, lightbars swirling. A show of force.

Mark's got two drinks in his hands, one liquor, one seltzer. Liquor's for me.

Mark sips the seltzer.

Looks like the mayor's decided to finally crack down.

Now? Why?

I think it's the Crusade. You must have heard about it. Harrow at the Garden.

You ever met him?

T. K. Harrow? Oh no. But I never really felt like we were in the same business, to be honest.

We watch as the cops lay down bright orange barricades.

What are they doing? Chasing them out?

No.

Another sip.

Sealing them in.

Persephone comes out of the bathroom, poured into snakeskin pants.

What do you think? Nice, right? Chinatown special. They're Prada. So cheap! I had to roll the waistband a little to get them on.

I unroll the waistband a little.

I hate to tell you this.

What?

They're not Prada. They're Prodo.

———

Mark agrees to let Persephone bunk for the time being. One thing you can say about Trump Tower, like most high-rises, the security is not lax. Two round-the-clock doormen, well armed, and private plainclothes patrolling the halls. If Pilot wants in here, he'll have to scale the outside of the building with a plunger in each hand.

I decide to head back to Hoboken. Mark hands me a card.

Give this to the driver. He'll take you. The Holland Tunnel's still functional, right?

I give Persephone a peck on the forehead.

Mark's good people. He'll take care of you.

Thanks. So who's going to take care of you?

That's what I'm heading back to Jersey to figure out.

Truth is, I have no idea what the next step should be. I've had jobs get out of hand, but not like this. I was hired to kill her, not adopt her.

And to be honest, I would have been happy to put her on a bus, point her north, deal with the fallout with Harrow myself. But that's not an option anymore. Not if I know that Harrow has also sent someone like Pilot.

Pilot definitely strikes me as a different kind of psycho.

So Persephone's problem is now my problem.

Which means Persephone is now my problem.

Though, I confess, it's more than that.

Sometimes when people call me, I can tell pretty soon that they don't want to hire me, they just want to chat. Blow off steam, fantasize, walk up to the edge but not over it. Before I hang up on them, they always throw out that same question.

Just tell me: How can you do what you do?

I don't answer, of course, but if I did, here's what I'd tell them.

It's not the doing-it part that's hard. It's the justifying-it part. And I don't do that.

I'm not the decision. I'm just the action.

I'm just the bullet.

So I don't need to justify it. Or live with it.

That's your job.

And there's one more thing I'd tell them.

The world is full of bullets. Sometimes in the form of speeding buses. Or aneurysms that go pop in the night. Or rotted branches that fall in a snowstorm at the exact moment you happen to pass.

Or exploding subways. Or bombs left in gym bags.

All bullets.

We dodge them every day, until one day we don't.

So if I didn't hang up, that's what I'd tell them.

That's how I do it.

I'm just another bullet.

But not this time.

Not for her.

When I get to the ground floor outside Mark's building I hand his limo driver the card and tell him to take me home.

First, though, we're making a detour.

Direct him straight down Broadway and he groans.

Drives as far as Fifty-Third, then pulls over and says he'll keep the engine running.

I can't begrudge a man his fears. So I get out and walk south.

Skirting the edge of Times Square.

I pass a few bored cops and a few hopeful clickers, decked out in their goggles and Geiger counters, sweeping the sidewalks for junk that's not too poisonous to pocket. Truth is, everything worth scavenging got snatched up years ago. All those toxic souvenirs.

I head east at Fiftieth.

Follow the faint hum of gospel.

It is still Sunday after all.

Half-wonder if I'll bump into Pilot. I figure I'm headed to either the last place he'll look for me, or the first.

Street's dark. Like a cellblock after lights-out.

Not Radio City, though.

Radio City is lit up like it's opening night.

On the marquee: The Crystal Corral Revival Hour.

Rockwell was right. Crystal Corral does sound like a country singer.

I head into the lobby and an usher intercepts me. Smiles and says I haven't missed much.

In the seats, maybe a thousand people, all huddled near the stage and singing softly.

Onstage, a giant screen.

On the screen, a giant preacher.

T. K. Harrow.

Head as high as a drive-in movie screen.

Sunday sermons broadcast on a loop. Free admission.

All welcome.

When Rockwell gave me his rundown, I didn't mention I'd been to this place before. Made a few visits right after Times Square, back when prayer suddenly seemed like a viable option. Churches or beds. Most people sampled.

Congregation sings the chorus.

So I'll cherish the old rugged cross. Till my trophies at last I lay down.

Harrow, in close-up, expounds the Word in urgent staccato. Sounds a fire-and-brimstone drumbeat under the melody of the hymn.

Usher taps me on the shoulder. Can't be older than twenty. Clean-cut. Cheap suit. But well kept.

Hello, brother. Care to join me down front?

No thanks. I'm just browsing.

Well, whatever you're looking for, you won't find it out there. In here, though, that's a different story.

I glance around. Shrug.

Awfully close to Times Square.

He smiles.

It's true. This city has a sick heart. But that poison can't touch you in here.

You sure about that?

Brother, it doesn't matter, because we're headed to a better place.

Sure. Of course, there's just one catch.

What's that?

You have to die first.

He hands me a pamphlet.

Not necessarily.

Claps my shoulder.

Our door's always open.

He leaves me, drifts toward the front, rejoins the chorus.

I will cling to the old rugged cross. And exchange it one day for a crown.

On the pamphlet's glossy cover, a photo of a rustic barn. Placid countryside. Golden sunshine.

Heavenly.

Arrayed over the barn, in bold letters:

PAVED WITH GOLD.

Under that. Bolder letters.

WHY WAIT?

I tap the bulletproof glass, startle the driver.

He seems happy when I point him toward Hoboken.

The limo glides down the west side, and for the first time in a long while, I feel a hard ache for the beds. Here in the backseat, it's almost like being on bed-rest: silent, safe, the low hum of movement with the city sliding by, untouchable, untouched, just lights.

When I get back to my apartment I find a padded envelope taped to my apartment door. I pry it loose, rip it open. Shake it out.

Aviators.

Lenses cracked. Blood-dotted.

Interesting.

I shake the envelope again.

Out comes a note.

Consider these an apology. Or a good-faith gift. Mr Harrow regrets our misunderstanding and he would very much like to meet with you. We hope to resolve this matter in a timely and amicable fashion. Please contact me directly at the number below.

The signature's from someone named Milgram.

I palm the note, pocket the shades.

Unlock my door.

I like that phrase.

Good faith.

II.

16.

We're in a wheat field.

Belt-high stalks rustle in unison, like a congregation on their knees, whispering prayers. I reach both my hands out to let the stalk tops and wheat flowers tickle at my palms.

T. K. Harrow walks beside me.

—and the most beautiful thing of it is, we can make of this what we wish. This realm is given to us as a second Eden. God made us once in His image, and now He's provided us the tools, and the know-how, to remake ourselves in His.

A white clapboard church on the crest of a hill.

Steeple bells welcome us.

Harrow hikes toward it, a half-step in front of me.

See, now this here is exactly the kind of church I grew up in. Small. Cozy. Everyone knew everyone. You couldn't look left or right there wasn't someone looking back at you, quick with a smile or a steadying word. I mean, don't get me wrong. I am thankful for my many blessings. But sometimes I think of what we've built today and wonder what we lost along the way.

The door is ajar. We enter. Rough-hewn pews on a wide-plank floor. Sunlight spun into stained-glass rainbows.

A vacant crucifix hangs heavy behind the pulpit.

Life-sized.

Harrow takes a seat in the front row and motions for me to join him.

I'm sorry we couldn't meet in person. But this is much preferable, don't you agree?

He could have self-presented in any way he chose. A serpent, the angel Gabriel, or simply T. K. Harrow forty years ago, still robust and full of hellfire. But he's here more or less as you'd find him in life, as he looked on that Radio City screen. Tall, weathered, bristly gray hair, scarecrow thin, a kindly face when it wants to be kind, but one that easily snaps back to rectitude. The only costuming flourish he allows himself is that on TV he's always in a suit. Here he's in flannels and wool. Work clothes.

As for me, I look like me. A garbageman.

Harrow claps me on the shoulder with a hand gnarled by age, his fingers folded up like a wounded bird. Still, his grip is strong.

When I was a lad, sitting on a pew not much more comfortable than this one, in a church pretty much just like this, the most terrifying thing to me in the whole wide world was not death, or the wages of wickedness, or the wrath of the Almighty Lord. It was the stares of Miss Savonarola.

Harrow chuckles at the memory.

She was our church organist. Tiny woman. Would sit at the electronic organ, right up there.

He points a crooked finger toward the altar.

She sat facing the congregation. Her eyes could just barely peer over the top of the organ. Yet I remember those eyes like twin glowing moons, hanging low on the horizon. And the funny thing about Miss Savonarola was that, before the service, she was your favorite person in the world. She'd greet you at the door and slip you sweets from her dress pocket, make you promise not to tell your folks. But during the service, let me tell you. She changed. You could hide in the back row, crouched out of sight, bury your toy in your lap, didn't matter. You got up to mischief while the pastor was preaching, she saw. She'd find you after the service and *whap!* Rap your wrists with a switch right in front of your parents. Wouldn't even say why, to you or to them. But she knew. And she knew you knew. And I will tell you, Mr Spademan. I am respectful and awed by my Lord in His heaven, but I don't think anyone's ever kept me in line better than she did. She taught me a few things, I'll tell you that.

I can imagine.

I understand you're not much one for this spectral world, am I correct?

That's right.

Have you ever been off-body before?

Long ago. Gave it up.

I understand. As with any dream, a lot depends upon the dreamer. Well, you've seen a little of what my dream looks like. But let me lay it out for you. I want to lead my followers here, to this world, a refuge of simplicity and peace. A sanctuary of my own devising.

He sweeps his hand over the church. Through the windows, sunlight sneaks in, pools in the corners, keeps to itself.

You know what's become of the world back there, Mr Spademan. You better than anyone. It is not a place to waste your days. How you live in that poisoned swamp of New York City, I will never understand. Not when you could live here. Like this.

Mr Harrow, I get that. I do. But why do people need to sign on to your dream? People should dream how they like.

Because I offer them something better. More than the dream. I offer them a new life, Mr Spademan. A life after life. With no wait list. Something remarkable. That is what I wanted to show you. Do you have time for a short demonstration?

Sure.

Harrow gestures to someone unseen. Two girls walk in through a side door. Identical twins, short hair, bright eyes. Persephone's age or a few years younger. Dressed in matching pinafore smocks. Prairie-style.

They stand before us, shoulder to shoulder, like soldiers awaiting inspection.

This is Mary and Magdalene. Go ahead, Mr Spademan. I want you to stroke Mary's cheek. She's the one on the right. Don't worry. She won't bite.

I reach my hand out and pass my knuckles lightly over her downy cheek. Soft. She giggles.

Very good. And now Magdalene.

Same thing. Knuckles grazing. On this pass, though, I get a little charge.

The first cheek was like experiencing the memory of something. Like a reminder of a feeling you once had.

The second one is like feeling it for the first time.

I settle back into the pew.

What do you think, Mr Spademan? As real as real. And that is my proprietary technology. You can't get that in any other dream.

He dismisses the twins. They curtsy and exit, like it's the end of a school pageant.

I'm still rubbing my hand.

That's very convincing.

That it is.

So what's the secret?

Just that. A secret.

Well I'm sure it will prove very lucrative.

Wait. There's one more person I want you to meet.

He stands.

You might want to stand up for this.

I stand.

And in she walks.

My Stella.

17

My wife.

In the same dress I last saw her in. She smiles.

That smile.

Brown hair in a bob. That bob I begged her not to get.

Looks good on her though.

I grasp Harrow's arm. For balance.

He gives me the satisfied look of a salesman who's just unveiled the luxury model.

I assure you, it's perfectly safe. It's not the real, no. But it's as real as real.

I look at her.

Her.

Here.

Brown eyes a little too close together. Front teeth a little too far apart. That smile that's spring-loaded to burst into a laugh.

In other words, perfect.

Don't be shy, Mr Spademan. Please give your wife a kiss. This is a place of sanctuary. And I promise to avert my eyes.

I turn to Harrow.

Shut it off.

Don't be afraid.

No. This isn't real.

I think you'll find, Mr Spademan, that those kinds of distinctions quickly become immaterial.

I turn back to her. Trembling.

Tell myself it's not real.

It's not real. It's not real. It's not real.

As I say this I take her face in my hands.

Feel her face.

Hesitate.

Kiss her.

Like a man drawing breath after years underwater.

I pull away.

I whisper.

I'm sorry.

Harrow lays a gentle hand on my back.

You understand now? What I am offering?

My Stella smiles. Her hand trails my face.

Don't worry, Mr Spademan. She will always be here. And I can arrange for you to see her whenever you like. In total privacy. Frankly, if you choose, you can leave that toxic world behind and relocate here, if that's what pleases you. You won't be the first. I know you're familiar with my farm. I can reunite you and your wife and I guarantee, after a time, you won't remember that you ever weren't together.

So this is what you're offering?

Yes.

And I'm guessing you'll want something in return.

Only something that is already mine.

Sounds fair. Just one question.

Anything.

Not for you. For her.

I turn back to face my Stella. Her look says she longs for me.

I choke back something. Then say it.

What's my name?

She smiles.

Spademan.

I smile back.

No, it's not.

She looks confused. Says it again.

Spademan.

I turn back to Harrow.

I want out.

He waves her away. The sales pitch gone sour.

She retreats out the side door. I can't help but watch her.

The door closing behind her.

Just like that last morning.

Then she's gone.

I lean on the pew. Struggle to get my balance. Fail.

Look at Harrow.

Tap me out.

Mr Spademan—

Now.

—I know it can be very overwhelming. It reminds me a bit of that first moment after baptism. When people come up again out of the water. Gasping for air, fighting for balance. But new. Brand-new. Like newborns. Come into a new life.

But it's not real.

No. But after awhile, I assure you, that hardly matters.

I want out.

He grasps my shoulders to stand me up. Steadies me.

All right. But first, let me tell you what I want.

His smile exiled.

I want my daughter back.

I don't know where she is.

He laughs.

Lying is not an effective tactic in this world. Not with me. And you should be wary of breaking commandments. Here, of all places, in the Lord's house. We certainly don't want to start down that road.

What road?

Breaking things.

I can't do it.

She is of no consequence to you.

Doesn't matter.

Mr Spademan, do you understand what I'm offering you?

Yes.

And why exactly are you protecting my daughter?

I don't know.

Do you even know why my daughter ran away?

I have some idea.

Do you? Well, let me fill in the blanks.

Harrow retreats to the pulpit and pulls down the massive leather-bound Bible. He opens it and flips onionskin pages.

I wipe my mouth, still unsteady. Sit.

I'm not in the mood for a parable, Mr Harrow.

He looks up.

That's not what this is.

He turns the book around. Upends it, cradling it in his arms, held toward me. Like it's story time.

On one page, the usual march of verses under a single illuminated letter, painstakingly painted.

On the other page, a large photo of Persephone naked.

This is my daughter, Grace Chastity. Whom I raised from an infant, as you know. Whose diapers I changed. Whose blankets I tucked in. Whose cries in the night I comforted.

He flips the page. More Grace Chastity. More naked.

Girls grow up. I understand that. And mine did too. All of them. Especially Grace.

He flips the page. In each photo, Grace is smiling, posing,

puckering her lips. In most photos there's a starburst of a cameraphone flash. In each one she is exposed. In some more exposed than others.

My Grace found a boyfriend, as little girls do. They break their fathers' hearts eventually. But I caught my Grace sending these pictures to her boyfriend. Shaming herself. Before him. Before me. Before God.

Flips the page again. A homemade porn mag, starring his daughter. In the next shot, she's on a bed, legs spread. Fingers finding their way inside her.

So you can imagine, Mr Spademan, that when I found these I was very cross. Very cross indeed.

Flip. Next photo. Shot from behind. Displaying a gymnast's agility. Among other things.

You don't have a daughter, do you?

No.

But you can understand how this might make you feel.

Sure. But she's eighteen. She's free to live her own life. Should be, anyway.

Well, she wasn't eighteen when she took these, Mr Spademan. She was sixteen. And she promised me she'd stop. More recently, she broke that promise to me. Again.

Flip. Young Grace Chastity explores sex toys. Makes them disappear.

Do you know how I found these? A parishioner. A member of my own congregation. He came to me and told me his son had brought them to him. They'd been circulating. At his school.

He closes the book. Mercifully.

So I forbid her from seeing her boyfriend. Forbid her from having a phone. I forbid her from doing just about anything I could think of. And naturally, as young girls do, when the devil has their ear, she ran away.

He replaces the book on the altar.

You'll forgive the dramatics of my presentation. I just want to make sure you understand why I want her home. Whatever she's done to break my heart, break my rules, to humiliate me in public, to taint my congregation and flout God's commandments, I know she will be safer with me, in my care, than rambling around out there, living hand-to-mouth, in the gutters of New York. So I want my daughter back. You've already seen what I can offer in return.

You know she's pregnant.

Yes. Another souvenir of the boyfriend. A worthless sort.

That's not what she told me.

What are you suggesting, Mr Spademan?

That the father is right here in this church.

Really? An immaculate conception, then?

Not exactly.

Harrow clutches the sides of the pulpit. Enters full-on preacher mode. His cadence sounds something like Mark Ray, but soulless. The stern father, not the kind shepherd, sowing brimstone, not comfort.

He starts in.

For, lo, the wicked bend their bow, they make ready their arrow upon the string, that they may privily shoot at the upright in heart. But ask yourself this, Mr Spademan. How pregnant is my daughter? And when exactly did she run away? Not long ago, correct? A few weeks, maybe? Why, we only just contacted you last week.

He's right.

He goes on.

So in your version of the story, this foul act was committed, and she—what? Lived under my roof for another few months? And then suddenly one day woke up and decided to flee? Does that make much sense to you?

He's right again. It doesn't.

He goes on.

Well, let me provide you with an alternate version. In an act of brash but not uncharacteristic youthful rebellion, prompted by my admittedly severe punishments for her extremely humiliating acts of licentiousness, she had a foolish encounter with her no-good boyfriend. Which she managed to hide from me. For a time. When she could no longer hide it, she ran.

Which is when you contacted me.

That's correct.

And now you want her back.

Yes, I do.

Hmmm. Well, that does make more sense, I guess.

I'm glad you're starting to see the whole picture, Mr Spademan.

Sure. There's only one thing I don't quite get. And you'll have to forgive me. I can be a little dim sometimes.

And what is that?

You hired me to kill her, Mr Harrow. Not bring her home.

He smiles.

Someday you may know how it feels to be a father. You want to protect them, even from themselves. In any way you can.

Yeah. Well. I'm not buying it. But thanks.

The plain fact, Mr Spademan, is that someone in my security department overstepped his authority. That individual has been reprimanded severely, as you know. I believe you received a souvenir of that disciplinary action just recently.

So now you want her back. Like the Prodigal Daughter. Just like that.

Something changed my mind, Mr Spademan. I saw the light, as it were.

Really? What was that?

I learned I had a grandchild. That altered my way of seeing things. But I wouldn't expect you would understand something like that.

No.

I would never harm that child. No matter his provenance. Or the circumstances of his conception. I want that child back. I want both my children back.

And you won't hurt Persephone?

You mean Grace? Of course not. I just want her back in my arms.

Well, that's a very good sermon, Mr Harrow. And I do thank you for your time and the tour. And I'm sorry. I am. But I don't think I can do that. She's a grown woman and I'm not a truant officer. I only provide one service, and if you're no longer interested in that service, we should probably just go our separate ways.

Harrow steps down from the pulpit.

All right. I understand. You clearly see yourself as a man of principle. I respect that. However misguided.

I stand up.

I want out. Now. I'm tapping out. Unplug me.

I know you are new to the off-body experience, so let me explain how this works. This is my church. My construct. My world. You are my guest. And you'll wake up when I wake you up.

The light pooling in the church's dusty corners dries up. The stained-glass sunbeams snuff out.

The church door creaks behind us. All the way open. Then all the way closed.

I told you I learned a lesson from my dear old Miss Savonarola, yes? Do you want to know what that lesson was?

I glance back over the pews. Three gentlemen approaching up the aisle. Two are huge, wear overalls, and look like farmhands who bulk up by eating other farmhands.

The third is a black man. Trim build. Trim beard. Shoulders as wide as a roadblock.

I look back at Harrow.

What was the lesson?

He smiles.

First the sweets. Then the switch.

18.

I'm not much of a brawler and this one's over in a blink. Harrow's world, Harrow's rules, so I'm like a twelve-year-old fighting high-school bullies in a wading pool.

After a few good kidney shots, one of the farmboys gets behind me, loops his arms in under mine, kicks my knees out, and bends my arms back like butterfly wings.

Pinned.

I dangle.

The black guy steps to center stage.

Mr Spademan, hello. Pleased to meet you. They call me Simon the Magician. I am Mr Harrow's head of security.

Sure. I've heard of you.

Good.

I'm going to guess you're not a real magician.

I don't do card tricks, if that's what you mean.

He holds up a fist. Shows it to me. No tattoos. Just fist.

Pow.

Recocks.

But I do have this one nifty trick that I like.

Shows me the fist again. Tightens it like he's crushing coal.

The skin starts to grow over the gaps between his fingers.

Thumb absorbed into knuckles to make bigger knuckles.

His fist reborn as a wrecking ball of bone.

His world. His rules.

The Magician pulls the fist back. Lets it fly. Like the plunger in a pinball machine. My head's the pinball.

The left comes right after. Right left right, like a ball between bumpers.

I hear ringing.

Harrow's delivering a sermon from the pulpit.

Simon the Magician was a contemporary of Jesus. Also called Simon the Sorcerer, Simon Magus, occasionally Simon the Holy God.

While Harrow goes on with the history lesson, Simon's namesake lets another loose across my chin. He might be named for some magician, but like Samson, he's got a thing for jawbones.

Harrow preaches.

Simon the Magician was a miracle-worker. He was considered the most powerful holy man in Samaria. Some thought him a deity. That is, until Jesus came along.

Simon stands over me, legs spread in a fighting stance. Fists hover like bees outside a hive, looking for the way in. He's not much for words but he puts his two cents in. Simon says:

When I heard about him, I took to him immediately.

Right cross.

Simon says:

I like to think of him as the alternative Jesus.

Left cross.

Simon says:

You know. Black Jesus.

Right cross. Ah, the old rugged cross.

Harrow bangs on the pulpit with the flat of his hand.

And do you know what Simon the Magician did, Mr Spademan, once he was upstaged by the one true Lord?

I wonder if I'm expected to answer. I was always taught not to talk with my mouth full of teeth.

Harrow plows on.

He converted. Followed Jesus. A convert, Mr Spademan. A smart man.

Farmboy lets me drop like a feed sack.

I cough. Dribble blood.

You made your point. Wake me up.

I can't do that, Mr Spademan. As real as real, am I right?

Harrow steps down from the pulpit. Toes me with a work boot.

I spit on the boot. Blood-colored polish. Spit-shine.

You may as well put your suit back on, Harrow. I'm guessing the country charmer portion of the program is over.

The pity is, Mr Spademan, that we can't kill you in here. You can't die. It's not possible. Most times that seems like an inconvenient impediment. But sometimes it proves surprisingly useful.

Simon stomps my head. I'm really starting to hate this magic act.

Mr Spademan, when I say we can do this all day, I really do mean it. All day. All night. A whole lifetime.

Simon stomps my head.

I spit up.

Harrow, I came here in good faith.

Harrow laughs.

Now what would you presume to tell me about faith, good or otherwise?

Simon stomps my head.

Skulls weren't made for this.

Harrow stands over me, supervising like a pit boss watching a card sharp get his comeuppance.

I want my daughter back.

———

Knock at the church door.

Some minutes later. Not sure how many. Several stomps' worth, at least.

Harrow looks at Simon. Simon looks at Farmboy Number One. Who looks at Farmboy Number Two. Who walks over and answers the door.

Enter Mark Ray.

I look up from the wide-plank floor. Taste of plank in my mouth.

Mark's in some kind of getup. It all matches his blond curls nicely. White robe. Sandals. Gold braid belt.

Hurlbat.

Sorry to interrupt. Did I miss the sermon?

A hurlbat looks like an ax but with two blades, set in opposite directions, one east, one west. Mark grips it and twirls it loosely in a batting stance, like a slugger waiting on-deck. Farmboy Number One watches mutely.

So he gives Farmboy Number One a closer look.

Farmboy falls.

Mark pries the hurlbat free from the farmboy's face. It takes a couple of good jimmies to pry loose.

Ax free, Mark walks up the aisle.

Since we're telling religious stories, I've got a good one. Saint Fidelis. Heard of him? German saint. Philosopher. Friar. Wore a hair-shirt. You ever worn a hair-shirt? Anyone?

Farmboy Number Two shrugs. Harrow and Simon stand silent, sizing Mark up. Simon's fists turn back into hands. He spreads his fingers, cracks newfound knuckles.

Mark continues.

It's no fun, I'll you that. A hair-shirt I mean. Not recommended. Do you know the hair's on the inside? Anyway. Saint Fidelis. Scourge of heretics. Known to carry—

And here he bows and presents his weapon to each man like a jester proudly showing off his scepter.

—a hurlbat.

Then Mark stands. Shakes his shoulders out. Regrips. Crouches once, a quick low bounce in the knees, then sticks the ax into the middle of Farmboy Number Two.

Timber.

I'd give him a standing ovation if I could stand.

Harrow steps forward.

And who are you?

I'm just here to pick up my friend.

We're having a word with him.

So I see. Don't worry. I'm not here to stop the hurting. I'm just here to spread it around a little bit.

He takes a quick step left and hacks toward Simon, who feints, snatches the handle, twists, and wrests it free.

Mark empty-handed.

Harrow smiles.

All right. Now we can talk like civilized folk. May I ask, and I apologize if this sounds somewhat silly given the situation, but how the devil did you manage to get in here?

Funny you should mention that. I know a devil. From Chinatown. Name's Rick.

Well. That's all very interesting, Mr—

Uriel.

Apparently Mark's got a nickname.

Mr Uriel. But this is still my construct. Yes? My church. My rules.

That's true. More or less.

So I'm afraid I'm going to have to ask you to leave.

Harrow gestures to Simon, who steps up, ax held high.
Ready to swing low.

Mark's robe ripples in the back.

Rips.

Mark's flesh ripples in the back.

Rips.

Mark lurches forward.

Mark's a hunchback.

Then an angel.

Wings unfurl.

Ax meets air.

Mark's foot meets Simon's forehead. Hard. From on high.

Mark's airborne. He laughs.

Turns his sandal into a steel-toe boot.

Kicks Simon again. Harder.

For unto you is given this day a boot to the head.

Simon staggers.

Harrow waves his hand.

All right. Enough.

He toes me.

Simon, tap out Mr Spademan.

Harrow looks up at Mark, who hovers, feathered wings
trembling.

I imagine you can find your own way out.

19

I'm awake. In a bed. In a cathedral.

Not a cathedral. A bank.

An angel hovers over me.

Not an angel. A nurse.

Behind her, Mr Milgram. He of the note.

The nurse cradles my face.

Be still. Let the painkillers work.

My jaw and skull throb. Nothing broken but a very convincing facsimile.

Pain. Killers.

Two things I've been spending way too much time with recently.

We're in the financial district, the old Wall Street, where I came to meet Milgram, a neighborhood where abandoned banks abound. This one's got vaulted ceilings, like a burial vault, built for kings. Paintings on the ceiling. Angels touching men.

Milgram hands me a card.

Mr Harrow would like you to know his offer still stands.

Milgram's a fussy type. Buttoned-down. Looks like he'd enjoy the back room at the Bait & Switch. Though I'm not sure which end of the whip he'd prefer.

I take the card.

One question.

Yes?

Why hire me if you'd already sent Pilot?

Mr Pilot's job wasn't to kill her. That was your job. Mr Pilot's job was to kill you. So, as you can see, this has been a real cavalcade of incompetence. But rest assured, we plan to set it right.

I stash the card.

Don't expect a call.

He tries to grin, can't quite make it past a wince.

Well, I suspect you'll be hearing from us either way.

I stop outside on the stone steps of the bank. Sit on the steps. Catch my breath.

Run a palm over the cold pebbled stone, squinting at the street, which is all edges and angles and light.

It's early morning. New day still has that new-day smell. Sunlight scrubs away what's left of last night. Tries to, anyway.

I don't go off-body often and haven't in a long while.

It's been long enough that I forgot about this part.

Bed-resters call it the wake-up call. A painful sensitivity when the simulation's over and you first come out of it and your senses all come back online. When you're back to using your actual organs, your eyes and ears and nose and nerves all open for business again.

Light searing your optic nerves. Odors numbing your nose. Sound galloping across your eardrums.

The wake-up call.

It's painful. Everything seems too real for a time.

The too-sharp edges of the actual world.

20

I collect myself and take the 2 train north toward Trump Tower. There are so few passengers at this hour they only run four cars to a train. And there's no such thing as express anymore. Everything's local. Making all stops. Except Times Square.

We rattle through without braking.

Times Square sealed off like a crypt.

The first explosion was small, on the subway, a diversion. Gym bag in the first car of a Manhattan-bound train. Intended to draw first responders down into the tunnel. Ambulance, EMS, fire crews, which it did.

Then came the second explosion.

The dirty bomb in Times Square went off about an hour after that.

Chaos opened the door to chaos.

Like a burglar sneaking in a side window, then unlocking the front door for his friends.

It was midmorning, Monday, holiday season. Just starting to get cold.

I remember they'd lit the big tree the week before. Local weatherman flipped the switch.

My Stella always liked to go into Manhattan to see the Christmas windows. She didn't mind braving the holiday crush, standing twenty-deep in a spillover crowd. She had a taste for magic. Silver snowflakes and mechanical elves, shilling name-brand gifts. Santa's helpers, doing the robot, that was always my joke.

She used to talk about us renting a little flat in the Village. Nothing fancy, but on a pretty street. With trees. The city had a pull on her that I didn't share. But she'd read all the romantic memoirs. The ones about a city rich with artists and poets and dreamers, the old-fashioned kind.

In my more sour moods, I'd remind her we were about a hundred years and a million dollars too late.

Irony is, pretty soon we could have had our pick.

That morning she watched me empty a pint bottle into the toilet bowl and made me promise it was the last time, for the last time.

She thought the drinking had something to do with the baby, or more to the point, the not-baby. Our inconceivable child. We're looking to trade one bottle for another, is how she put it. That was always her joke, when she was in the mood for joking.

So I poured out the last bottle and swore never again on various graves. Truth was, I just wanted her to leave. I had an appointment to keep that morning.

Besides, it was easy enough to kick the bottle.

By that time I'd discovered the beds.

They drove it straight down from upstate, down the Henry Hudson, left at Forty-Second, right into Times Square, no stops. Made the whole trip on one tank of gas.

Officials later said if they hadn't blown themselves up they would have died in a few months anyway, just from handling the radioactive waste. Maybe if they'd had second thoughts. Dithered while they withered away in a quiet farmhouse somewhere.

The world's first long-term suicide bombers.

But they didn't. They drove it straight into the heart of Manhattan. Like a stake.

A van stuffed with a bomb stuffed with fertilizer salted with waste lifted from a radiotherapy clinic in foreclosure. Enough to poison twenty city blocks.

Crude stuff. But somehow fitting.

A bomb made of shit and someone else's trash.

Pulled to a stop outside a TGI Fridays.

Whispering a final fevered prayer.

Back doors blew open and gave birth to a toxic cloud.

Shattered windows. Splattered tourists.

Glass. Blood. Sirens. Smoke. Screams.

Hair. Bones. Ashes. Skin. Flesh.

Charnel carnage.

Almost biblical.

A loosed plague.

We fought that morning, like many mornings, like most. I was back from my leave, back at work but not really, and not often. And she was just starting to realize that Broadway was a lot more crowded than a high-school stage in Jersey.

Still, she went to her classes, and to her auditions, and failed, then came home and we went to bed, and failed at that too.

So the rest of the time we fought.

At least that we were good at.

———

Times Square closed for cleaning and never reopened. They kept telling us the radiation wasn't that bad. You can easily endure small exposures, they said. No worse than a few X-rays at the dentist.

The city issued handheld Geiger counters for free. Became a bit of a hip accessory for a time. Cool young kids clickety-clicking their way through the city, counters slung around their necks like tourists' cameras. Even turned into a popular pickup line. Approach a young woman. Hold up your Geiger counter.

Whoa, I think I've found a hot spot.

Crafty vendors pitched card tables on sidewalks around the city, swapped out I Love New York t-shirts for I Survived Times Square. Set out rows of little plastic glow-in-the-dark Empire State Buildings and Statues of Liberty, a tiny toxic skyline. Funny idea, sick but funny, but there were no tourists around to buy them. And no native wanted an I Survived Times Square shirt when you couldn't really be sure yet that you had.

The mayor preached calm. As a stunt, he sat down for dinner in the middle of empty Times Square, ate a five-course meal with his wife. Silverware, candlesticks, white-coated waiters, white linen tablecloth, violinist, the whole thing. Dabbed his mouth with a napkin, turned to the TV cameras, proudly declared: Tell the world.

New York is open for business.

Didn't matter. The tourists never returned. That's a hard sell, even with three-for-one specials on hotel suites. All the businesses failed. They were built on selling M&M's and I Love New York shirts to visitors. Problem was, no one was hungry for candy and no one loved New York anymore.

The violinist came down with a rare sarcoma and died the following Easter. The mayor sent an aide to the funeral.

Dirty bomb killed all the dogs in the city too. All of them.

No one's ever figured that one out.

The president came. Made a speech from a safe distance. Reminded us that America always rebuilds. Recovers. Rises again.

Then he rose again. In a helicopter.

A couple of weeks later, the first car bomb went off. Near the United Nations.

People watched live on the news and hoped it was just a faulty taxi, burst into flames. That kind of thing used to happen.

People watched and hoped. Until the second one went off. Took out the news crews.

Then a few days later, another. Then another.

Over the next few weeks.

Not often. But often enough.

The president made another speech, this time from the Oval Office. Preempted football during half-time, sent his condolences and ordered in the National Guard. Promised the country was behind us, we'd spare no effort in seeking justice, then signed off with a God Bless America and God Bless New York, just in time for the second-half kickoff.

Every day, right before she'd leave to face another parade of smiling rejections, she'd stand and steel herself at the front door, hand poised on the first of the locks.

Beyond that door was the fiery furnace. We had to trust together that each day we wouldn't be consumed. Burned up. Venture out on faith.

Like that old Sunday school story.

Me Shadrach. Her Meshach.

Still hoping for an Abednego.

And every day my Stella said the same strange thing, paused there at the door.

Said it mostly to herself.

See you on the other side.

Every day she said that.

Even the last one.

Within a month Times Square was dead and rotting, beyond resuscitation, and the rot spread out in circles from there.

But by that point no one cared. It's not that we didn't care about the attacks. We were New Yorkers, after all. Battle-scarred. We rattled our swords. We gathered in the streets, held candles, demanded justice. Demanded vengeance. We knew how this worked, we'd done it before. We hounded the brown-faced. Jumped a few Sikhs in our ignorance. A few Brazilians. Gave gay-bashers license once again to work out their issues on swarthy civilians. We were indiscriminate in our discrimination.

It wasn't that we didn't care about the bombings. We just didn't care about the city. Not really. Not that part. Not those streets. Most native New Yorkers, to be honest, had abandoned Times Square long ago. Thought of it mostly as a tourist preserve. Cursed the bright neon signs, the Naked Cowboy, and whatever errands might bring you there on a crowded Saturday to fight through the sluggish global herd.

It wasn't long before native New Yorkers were all making the same grim jokes. Times Square? Roach bomb. Ha-ha-ha. Or, Times Square? I've heard it really glows at night. Or,

Times Square? They finally figured out a way to get a tourist to step aside on the sidewalk. Or, Times Square? They bombed it? Well, who among us hasn't thought of doing that at least once?

But the reality was that the walls had been breached and the tourists stopped coming and the streets emptied out and soon the rest of the people started packing up too. Some skyward, to glass penthouses and the lure of the limnosphere. Most just outward, to some other city without a toxic tumor in its midsection.

The car bombs didn't help.

America's big, and the long recession had hollowed out most of the rest of the East Coast, so it wasn't that hard to up and move, to find another house, on another block, in another neighborhood, another job, another chance, in another city that wasn't suddenly halfway poisonous. Where you didn't have to stand and sniff the wind each morning from your doorway and try to gauge just how much death you could smell in the air, and whether today it was blowing toward you.

"Incremental Apocalypse" became the term of choice. Coined by some newspaper columnist, in an angry rant about the city quietly dying.

No zombie overrun. No alien armada. No swallowing tsunami. No catastrophic quake.

Just the gradual erosion of the will to stick it out.

A trickle became a stream became a torrent became an exodus.

So, sure, Times Square?

Times Square didn't kill too many New Yorkers.

But it killed New York.

———

The day it happened, I was in Chinatown sleeping.

Deep in a custom-made dream.

Stooped over, wringing my hands in a waiting room.

Then slapping backs and unwrapping cigars.

Bright blue balloons kissing the ceiling.

Congratulations all around.

My wife died in that first one, the one on the subway. The small one.

The diversion.

On her way to acting class.

In the months after I could only hope she was riding in the first car. I hope she was standing right next to the bomb. I hope she picked up that damned gym bag, unzipped it, poked her head in, right before it detonated.

I hope it blew her to dust.

I hope that she didn't lay wounded, twisted, in the dark-, ness of that tunnel, waiting for sirens, waiting for help, hearing them carefully make their way down, advancing step-by-step through the wreckage, then die in the second explosion.

Everyone who was left died in the second explosion.

I hope she died in the first one. The diversion.

That's what passes for hope these days.

21

On my way back to Mark's I make a detour to Hell's Kitchen. Radio City's too expensive to rent out on anything but Sundays, so Harrow has a Paved With Gold outreach center here, set up in a tidy storefront which is yawning awake just as I arrive. Strapping gents set out the pamphlet rack, while a wholesome blonde in a knee-length skirt sparks up the coffeemaker. Everyone has the whiff of missionary. Look too healthy to have been in New York for long.

I spot the clean-cut usher from the other night. Not in his suit now. Sharp slacks and a flowered Hawaiian. Looks like a Beach Boy.

I sit down in a folding chair opposite his desk.

Uncrease my brochure.

Tell me more.

I get the full pitch:

Fully subsidized dreaming on a pastoral country campus, a hundred acres, wholly owned and maintained by Crystal Corral Ministries. In essence, you sign on to serve the church, maybe do a tour of service in an urban outreach center like this one, maybe work some time doing labor on the Paved With Gold farm. For example, he says, he's from out west, California, and after this month-long stint in our fair city he's heading straight to Paved With Gold to tap in for the first time. Moreover, he assures me, the tours of duty are short and the requirements minimal. In fact, the church has had such a good response, he says, leaning in, beckoning me forward, like we're buddies and he's letting me in on a secret deal, they can't find enough work for all the applicants.

So some people get to go straight to heaven.

Do Not Pass Go, etcetera.

As for heaven: He hasn't been yet so he can't presume to describe it. But it's wholly scriptural, a hundred percent accurate, designed according to biblical teaching. You can visit for a day, a week, a month, he says, it's the ultimate time-share. I can tell he's used that line before.

Like a good salesman, he hasn't mentioned cost. So I mention it. Plead poor.

I'm just a garbageman.

He laughs.

Look at me. Think I'm a billionaire? Economy the way it is? And trust me, California is even worse.

Leans in again.

There is no cost.

How can that be?

He tents his fingers. I can tell this is his favorite part of the pitch.

Pastor Harrow pays the freight. With the money he raises through the church. Heaven should not require a golden ticket, as he likes to say. Just a golden heart.

This same quote runs across the bottom of the brochure.

The Beach Boy continues.

Think of it like the Army. They sign up thousands and it costs nothing to join. In fact, they pay you. Well, this is like that. It's God's army. There's no point in building a heaven if you haven't got anyone to walk its golden streets. That's Pastor Harrow also.

I figured.

I'll tell you this. You sign up today, I can have you at our farm by this time tomorrow. Morning after that, you'll wake up in Glory Land.

And where is all this exactly?

The Crystal Corral compound. South Carolina. Beautiful site.

Seems far.

From this? Are you kidding? I can't wait to get out of this hellhole. No offense.

I stand up. Tap the brochure on the desk.

I'll think about it.

When you make up your mind, we'll be here. Maybe not me, but definitely someone who can help you. But I'll be gone. I've got an appointment to keep.

Appreciate your time.

No worries. God bless you.

I figure the Beach Boy for a greenhorn. Another round of soothing hallelujahs and he might have closed this sale. You let me wriggle off the hook too easy, rookie.

Then I turn around and notice the line behind me that's waiting for my spot in the chair.

22

By the time I get back to Trump Tower, Rick the tech-head is long gone and Mark's up and around, out of his bed, unplugged, wearing a robe, drinking a coffee. He pours me one and offers me a bagel.

Good morning, Spademan. I believe the last time I saw you, it was in a country church where you were moonlighting as a doormat.

Very funny. Thanks for that, though. I mean it.

Well, Rick and I figured you might need a cavalry.

You two do that often? Crash other people's private meetings?

Not as a rule. But if you ever need to do it, Rick is definitely the best. Knows how to find the seams and how to slip you through them. I did enjoy the look of surprise on their faces.

You mean the faces you didn't bury your little toy ax in?

Mark shrugs.

Hey, I may not be much help in this world, but when you spend enough time on bed-rest, you tend to pick up a few party tricks.

So that's what you do in there all day? Fly around and hack people to pieces?

No. That was special for you. Though I do like to spread my wings once in awhile.

I nod toward Mark's bed.

Luxury liner like that, why the hell do you ever go all the way down to Chinatown?

You know me. I like congregations. The comforts of a like-minded crowd.

Persephone pads out of the bedroom. Wearing sweatpants. Scratches at bedhead curls.

Good morning. What I miss?

Eyes my bagel.

God, I'm starving. Is there one of those for me?

I hand it over.

Nice sweatpants. What happened to snakeskin?

She frowns.

They split.

Given that I can now be fairly sure there are no professional killers actively stalking us, at least not in the nuts-and-bolts world, I decide to be nice and treat everyone to a proper lunch. Mark suggests we head to the shopping mall next door. It was built as a sparkling lure, baited with luxury goods, but it's not so luxurious anymore and no one's biting. A few fancy restaurants still survive, catering to the dreamers upstairs, sending up five-star takeout, but the stores have all shuttered, most of the mall's abandoned, and all that's left of the jewelry boutiques and clothing stores are faded poster ads, peeling behind glass, selling shiny stuff you can no longer buy at shops that are no longer there.

In their place, now there's squatters' stalls mostly, set up illegally, lining the mall in long rows in front of the emptied-out stores. Mall owners turn a blind eye, collect payments in cash, figure at least the street market keeps foot traffic up, wards off squatters who come in from the park. Figure all the old businesses packed up anyway, heading for higher ground. Let the nomads move in, pitch a tent. Plant a flag.

Many different flags, actually.

Vendors shout for attention as we pass, hawking wares,

stalls stacked with everything from dried spices to saris to sjamboks, those leather African half-whips, made as snake-killers and crafted from rhino hides, sold here for self-defense. That's the pitch anyway. Salesman demonstrates, slicing the air with a whistle as we walk. Cuts close to Persephone. She jumps, then curses. Salesman looses a goofy grin. She flips him double birds.

Then we head to the food court, which is just a cluster of food carts, run by guys who broke in the back way. Carts serve up dishes for a dollar, curries and dosas and kebabs. Flaming grills and sizzling griddles. The tempting scents of spiced steam. Everything looks delicious, though a few carts offer meats you wouldn't want to know the family tree of. Luckily all the vendors have the same strict food policy: No Questions Answered.

We retire to a bench in the mall with hot meals on our laps, not a utensil between us, a war council with paper plates. I go to dig in when Mark bows his head to say grace. Persephone follows. I succumb to peer pressure.

Mark with his eyes closed.

Lord we thank you for this bounty we are about to receive.

At first I think he's making a joke.

Apparently not.

Lord and thank you for watching over us and keeping us safe so far. Let our actions on this day as on every day glorify your name in every way. Amen.

Amen.

Amen.

I take a bite and ask the obvious.

Okay, Harrow's shown his hand. So what's our brilliant plan?

Mark eyes Persephone.

She shouldn't be here for this.

It's okay. She can hear this.

Mark shoots me a look. This is the look that says he's probably a little more qualified than me in the arena of emotional counseling. He's right. But I don't budge.

She can hear this.

He frowns. Then proceeds.

All right. Well. There's three potential outcomes, as I see it. You give him what he wants. You kill him. He kills you. Those are the only options.

Persephone pipes up.

Or I can run. I've been running. You don't even need to know which direction I went.

Mark wipes his mouth.

That's not an outcome. That's a delaying tactic. Eventually this ends. In one of those three ways.

He looks to me.

You a baseball fan?

No. Jets fan. Not by choice. By blood.

Well, in baseball there's this thing the statisticians call the three true outcomes. It's the three possible outcomes of an at-bat that only involve the actions of the pitcher and the hitter, and none of the other players on the field. So they're considered the purest possibilities.

Okay. And they are?

Mark counts them out on his fingers.

A walk. A strikeout. A home run. That's it. The three true outcomes.

I think of lesson two of hauling garbage. You discard it. It discards you. Or you die.

Three true outcomes.

Okay. I got it. So?

Mark pauses, then gives me a look. This is the look that says he's about to tell me something he doesn't want to tell me.

Go on, tell me.

There's another factor.

What's that?

This Simon. The Magician.

What about him?

He's a factor.

Because?

For starters, he's between you and Harrow.

I can take care of him.

Like you did in that church?

That's not fair. That was in there. That's the dream. We're out here now.

Even so.

I'm on better footing out here.

Still. I'm just saying. He's a factor.

You don't even know what he can do out here. Or who he really is. He could be eighty years old, for fuck's sake.

My guess? He's not.

So I turn to Persephone.

What do you know about him?

Simon? You saw him.

And?

He is what you think he is.

Meaning?

He's that bad. He's worse. Out here? He's worse.

Mark chimes in.

What about money? Can he be bought?

She laughs.

If you're planning to outbid my father, that's not an auction we're going to win.

I press her.

Okay. So what is he not good at?

I don't know. Whatever it is, I haven't seen it. He's ruthless. He's smart. And he's not someone you can reason with. And don't expect any sympathy. Or mercy.

All right. No reason. No sympathy. No mercy. That narrows our options, at least.

Persephone runs both hands through her unkempt curls. Tugs at tangles that refuse to untangle. Looks down at her feet.

Then tells us something more.

He was my bodyguard.

For how long?

Until I ran.

So he's not a great bodyguard. At least there's that.

It wasn't his fault. He was supposed to protect me. He wasn't my babysitter. And I wasn't his prisoner.

And he did a good job? Of protecting you?

Sure. From everyone but my father.

Mark reaches out, takes her hands in his. Mark the former pastor. Knows ways to balm wounds.

I say to Mark:

I still want to hear your three true outcomes.

Sure. Yes. Three true outcomes, like I said. You give him the girl, he kills you, you kill him. Walk, strikeout, home run. Only the pitcher and the batter have a say in it.

Okay.

In this case, Harrow's the pitcher. You're the batter.

He motions to Persephone.

We're just the fielders.

Okay.

Meaning ultimately you have to decide.

Okay. In that case, I choose the home run.

All right.

Wait. So which one is that again?

Very funny.

I put my hand on Persephone's, lightly.

But that means you and I need to have a conversation.

Mark's apartment, an hour later. Two chairs pulled up by the picture window. Mark's run off to Chinatown, day trip to the land of Nod.

She and I watch the campers in the park.

Weird to think I was down there with them a few days ago.

Didn't sound like it was too much fun.

It had its ups and downs.

You know them. You lived with them. You think they'll last long in there? Police have it locked down. Nothing in, nothing out.

They'll last.

The thing I don't understand is, what exactly are they protesting?

They're not protesting anything. They just want to live in a different kind of world. Figured you have to start building it somewhere.

Sure, but why Central Park? Why not Woodstock? Or Utah?

Take a look at the park. At this city. At this moment. It's all kind of up for grabs, don't you think?

So you know what this means.

Yes.

You okay with it?

Time was, I thought I might do it myself. Dreamt about it.

Nothing happens unless you say it can happen.

I know. Thank you.

She folds her hands over her belly.

I didn't think it would end like this. I just wanted to get away.

Well, what he did, that's going to follow you. He's going to follow you.

I know.

And it's not like he'll give you up.

I know.

Before this goes any further, I need to get something straight.

Okay.

When I saw your father, he showed me pictures.

Okay.

Of you.

Okay.

Said you took them.

I did.

Said you sent them to your boyfriend.

I did. They weren't meant for public consumption, obviously. But you know teenagers. We're stupid sometimes. Trust the wrong people.

We all do that.

Did he tell you where he found them?

He said someone from the congregation brought them forward.

Hmmm. Well, that's bullshit. My father trolls for that trash all the time on the Internet. Just so happened, one day, he clicked a link, saw his own daughter. In among all the usual naked jailbait he prefers. Just bad luck, really. For me, anyway.

He also told me something else. That your boyfriend is the father.

A dry laugh.

No. That asshole fucked me over plenty, but not in that way.

Your father says it isn't his.

Well, what do you expect him to say?

I just mean that, if you're running for some other reason, whatever it might be, I need to know.

She straightens. If any of this is acting, her look right now would win the Oscar.

Wait, what are you saying? You want to send me back to him?

I need to know what made you run. Because you didn't run at first. When you found out about the baby. You waited. For a few months at least.

I was scared. My father has a long reach. As you know.

But then something made you leave.

Yes. That's true.

Gnaws her lip. Says to me, her voice catching:

Just tell me you'll protect me.

I'll protect you.

Say it again.

I'll protect you.

Say it again.

I'll protect you.

She turns. Tears poised on her lower lids, peering over the edge, like jumpers on a ledge.

Yep. Just what I thought. Sounds just the same coming out of your mouth as it does out of everyone else's.

Grace—

Don't.

I will. I swear. I'll protect you.

Jumpers teeter.

Don't make me go back to him. Don't make us.

If what you told me is true—

It's true.

—well, then, I don't think your father can be forgiven. At least not by anyone he's bound to meet on this Earth. Certainly not by me. And not by you.

She looks back out over the park.

You're right. When I found out, I stayed. I thought maybe he would forgive me. He would still love me, love us, if I stayed. So that wasn't why I ran away.

No?

Jumpers jump. Free fall. Straight plummet down her cheek. Followed quick by more jumpers. They're all jumping now.

She looks at me.

No. And it's not the most unforgivable thing he's ever done.

23

So at first the rough plan was, we hold tight until Harrow arrives in Manhattan, when we know he'll be here, he'll be tapped out, and he'll be walking among the living. Grace told me that on his New York trips, he likes to meet with his top donors, the ones he calls the Deacons' Circle, show them a little Christian love. Then, of course, there's the Crusade itself, with Harrow preaching in public to an overflow crowd. Yes, there will be a hundred bodyguards and twenty thousand witnesses.

I said it was a plan. I didn't say it was a good plan.

But we thought, maybe a sniper shot. Sideswipe the motorcade. Finagle a face-to-face, rush the podium, take him down in a kamikaze tumble.

That was the plan, such as it was. Until Persephone told me her story.

The rest of it.

The part she hadn't told to anyone.

So Persephone had a best friend. Rachel.

She was a few years younger than Persephone. More beautiful than Persephone too, at least to hear Persephone tell it.

Troubled girl. Lost her parents young.

Came to church with an aunt and uncle.

Caught Harrow's eye. A long while back.

He took an interest.

———

When Rachel was young, maybe ten, Harrow became a kind of surrogate father. He wasn't around much, given his schedule, but he provided for her. Showed her favor. She was over at the house enough that she and Grace became like sisters, more or less. They always joked that Grace was like Heidi, living carefree in the Alps, and Rachel was like Clara, the sickly cousin come to take the mountain air.

They grew up together. They got older.

She even warned Grace against dating that boy who asked for the photographs.

One night Harrow called Rachel into his study. She thought maybe he was going to talk to her about offering to help her with college. He'd always been so generous. Even so, that was still a few years away.

Instead he told her about this marvelous new ministry.

Paved With Gold.

I want you to be one of my very first angels, is how he put it.

He personally escorted her to the camp. She could barely believe it. The famous T. K. Harrow, with her on his arm. She never went to prom so this felt to her like prom night.

He delivered her to the doorstep and said he couldn't wait for her to come back and tell him just how real the new heaven he was building felt.

She entered the camp's main building, which was built to look like a barn. Sodium lamps floated in the dark rafters. Beneath them there lay a checkerboard of hundreds of white-sheeted cots. But only a dozen dreamers so far, tapped in here and there. My pilgrims, Harrow had called them. When she walked in, the nurses stood to applaud her. She'd worn the best dress she had.

Ironed it twice.

The empty beds laid out so lovingly. Kindly nurses to tuck you in under sheets that smelled like spring. A scent that was hard to place, maybe gardenias.

The tube slides in painlessly.

The nurse leans over and you say a prayer together. She wears a white folded cap, pinned to her hair, like an old-time nurse. She kisses your forehead. You assure her you'll see her again soon and tell her all about it. She says she sure hopes so, but she also tells you that, for a lot of people, when they get to heaven, they don't ever want to tap out again.

You smile, and get drowsy, your eyelids drop like a heavy curtain at the end of a play. And you swear to yourself in that last waking moment, even as you still feel the loosening grip of the nurse's hand slip away, that you hear the distant lullaby of harps, you're absolutely sure that you can.

At Harrow's personal orders they tapped her out temporarily and put her under quarantine in an adjacent infirmary, where Rachel lay for a few hours in locked restraints in a sick bed, wondering exactly which of these two worlds she was torn between was the horrible dream.

Normally no one would have been allowed to see her, but she got word out to Grace Chastity through a junior pastor who'd long harbored a crush on her. Grace Chastity still had some special privileges also, daughter of the minister and all.

At this point, Grace wasn't showing yet.

So when she got word she came to Rachel's room at night

and visited Rachel and Rachel said nothing. She just smiled and strained against her cuffs as Grace stroked her cheek and she cried.

Then Rachel asked Grace if she still carried that knife.

What are you talking about?

Please don't ask me anything. Just help me get out of here. Don't ask me why just please help me get out of here.

So Grace tugged at the locked restraining strap and then, thwarted, pulled from her boot the five-inch knife which she'd been carrying every day since that night when her father thundered drunkenly into her room, waving a tablet, bright with pictures of her, like he was Moses catching the fallen praying to the golden calf. The night that she'd reflexively clutched the covers to her chin, as though they offered some protection, rather than simply something else for him to strip away.

Grace sawed through the first restraint.

Rachel's right hand sprang free.

Then Grace circled the bed to cut free her other arm but she couldn't get the angle right on the restraint and Rachel said here let me have it I can reach it better than you can so Grace in a thoughtless moment gave her the blade.

And Rachel without hesitation slashed it brightly across her bound left wrist then plunged it into her chest, plunging and plunging, smiling at Grace Chastity and saying good-bye good-bye I love you I love you I hope I will see you again one day.

What Grace would clearly remember forever is how she plunged with such anger, as though to drive something out.

Saying let this blood wash me clean oh Lord please Lord as she bled red widely on the stiff white sheets, until her strength drained away and she was lost in the swallowing stain.

And Persephone stood over her, and she took back the blade, and she kissed her friend on the forehead, and wiped the blade clean, and then she ran.

24

I take the brochure from my pocket, unfold it, lay it out flat on the coffee table.

PAVED WITH GOLD.

WHY WAIT?

Change of plan.

No sniper shot. No side-on suicide motorcade collision. No kamikaze attacks, no stealthy slit from the shadows.

No surprises. No sudden oblivion.

Because Harrow needs to know.

He needs to know who. And he needs to know why.

I fold the brochure and hide it in my pocket and don't tell anyone this as we sit in Rick's Chinatown flat, his sofa as shapeless as a deflating dinghy, and the three of us, me, Rick, and Mark Ray, all trapped on it together like survivors on the first day of month number two, adrift at sea.

Persephone's pregnant. Persephone gets a chair.

Mina Machina, Rick's live-in, comes slouching out of the kitchen, slurping at something steaming in a bowl. She's got long hair and she's alarmingly skinny, so she looks like a long wooden stand built to hold up a black wig. The wig could use a brushing too.

She giggles at something only she hears or understands, then lets the hot bowl slip and spill with a clatter.

Classic tapper. Still dreaming.

She retrieves, then wrestles with, a mop, which in her hands looks like an identical twin held upside-down, hair shocked white.

I ignore her and lay out the plan to the room.

We need to find a way to get to Harrow while he's here in New York for his crusade. As Mark said, there's only two ways this ends. We either hand over Persephone or we convince Harrow to stop asking. We're going to go with the second one. I'll handle that part.

Mark shoots me a look. This is the look that says I'm lying, because he actually said there were three ways this could end. But I figured I'd leave out the outcome where Harrow kills me. In any case, that's for me to worry about.

I continue. Lay out phase two. The post-Rachel part of the plan.

Rick, we also need to find a way to gate-crash Paved With Gold. We need to get into Harrow's heaven and get everyone out. Everyone.

Rick looks perplexed. Sparks a cigarette.

You want to crash heaven and then send everyone home? Why do you want to shit on the picnic?

I wave the smoke away. Nod to Persephone.

We've got a pregnant lady here.

Rick looks at her. Looks at me. Really was hoping to finish that cigarette.

Stubs it out. Doesn't matter where. The whole apartment's an ashtray.

Sorry. My bad.

Just tell me if it's possible. Like what you did with Mark when I was tapped in with Harrow before. Slide someone in, uninvited.

Sure, crashing in one person is easy enough. Tapping out everyone else who's also in that construct? All at once? That's trickier.

I don't care if it's tricky. I want to know if it's possible.

Rick rubs his palms on his thighs. Looks lost without his cigarette. Then shrugs.

Sure. Anything's possible. Sort of.

And what do you need from us?

I need someone inside. I can tap people out one by one from out here. It's slow going. You have to find them and then sever the link. And it's a lot easier if the people inside know what's happening.

Meaning what?

Meaning I need someone in there to give them a nudge. You know, pinch me, I'm dreaming, that kind of thing. Also, it helps a lot if they actually want to leave.

I don't think we'll have to worry about that.

I turn to Mark Ray.

Okay. So that's you and me, Mr Angel.

Mark extends a consoling pastor's hand to squeeze my shoulder, like I've come to him for advice.

I hate to say this, friend, but last time we tried this, you flailed around in there like a fat kid in water wings drowning in the shallow end.

Then Mark pivots to Rick, like it's time for the grown-ups to talk.

I'll go in. I can handle that part. But are you sure you can crash me into Paved With Gold? That thing's got to be a vault.

Rick winces, wrinkling Chinese tattoos.

Hard to say. When I crashed that country church, I learned a lot about their protocols, and those tend to be consistent across the board. That's the good news. The bad news is, last time they weren't expecting us. I'm guessing that won't be the case this time around. Also, that country-church construct? That was a quickie one-off, whipped up for your meeting. Designed for guests, so it was easy to crash. This heaven place is guaranteed to be a much more complicated construct. More secure. Walls are much higher, so to speak.

Mina, still waltzing with the mop.

You gotta piggyback.

Ricks waves her off. Like a bad smell.

She repeats.

An octave higher.

You gotta piggyback.

I'm interested. So I ask Rick.

What's that?

Rick rubs his temples like he just got hit by the nastiest migraine ever, and that headache is now dancing with a mop in his kitchen.

Then he spreads out his thin fingers, covered in silver skull rings. One skull per finger, thumbs too. Sterling graveyard. Then he lays it out. In laymen's terms.

Despite what my beautiful life partner says, piggybacking is just a fucking stunt. Look, I'm a cocky asshole gizmo daredevil and even I don't do it anymore.

Sure. But what is it?

You slide someone in on someone else's dream, someone who's been invited into the construct. Basically slip them in before the door closes. But it's a very dumb thing to do.

Why's that?

You ever see kids on skateboards hitch rides on the back of buses? It's kind of like that, except with your consciousness. You fuck it up, you will skin your knee. Badly.

How badly?

Come by my place, I'll show you the room where I keep those people. They don't mix too well with the general populace anymore.

Tugs at a skull ring. Twists it. Continues.

Besides, definitely no one's going to invite either of you two into their heavenly clubhouse, so it's a nonstarter, since there's no one to piggyback in on—

Persephone speaks up.

I can do that.

What?

They'll invite me in. If I ask to meet my father—

I interject.

Absolutely not.

Mark looks at me.

It's not a terrible idea.

Let's set the bar for ideas a little higher than not terrible.

Mark persists.

Look, she can't get hurt in there. Not really—

There are a lot of things they can do to her. Even in there.

—but I'll go in with her, to protect her. I'll be the one to piggyback in. Rick—I mean, you can do that, right?

Rick thinks. Twists a silver skull. Then nods.

Mark turns back to me.

You've seen me in there. You know I can handle myself. Better than you can, in there. And she's the only one of us who can possibly convince Harrow to tap in for a meeting. And if the goal is to tap everyone out, people in there will trust her a lot more readily than they'll trust me. Harrow's daughter? They'll follow her out. Familiar face and all—

Sure. Familiar face of a disgraced runaway—

Spademan, think about it. She lures Harrow in for a meeting. I follow her in and we take care of everyone in there. You find Harrow in his bed and take care of him out here. It's the only way this works—

No, Mark. I said absolutely—

Persephone cuts me off. Fiercely.

Look, I am very grateful for all that you've done for me, but I'm not your fucking daughter. I'll do what I want. And I'm doing this. I need to.

There is a long silence. During which we all listen to the stillness of Chinatown.

Broken finally by Mina's best Axl Rose falsetto.

Mop becomes a mike stand.

Knock knock knocking on heaven's door.

I figure it's time to call the meeting to a close.

So. New plan.

We break into heaven, set everyone free, lure in Harrow himself by dangling his runaway daughter, secretly slip Mark in behind her somehow, using some technique that Rick, the cockiest gizmo in Chinatown, isn't even sure is possible, they give Harrow a good talking-to, make him see the error of his wicked ways, perhaps offer up an apology to the daughter he fucked and maybe probably knocked up, all while I'm out here tracking down his flesh-and-bone body in the nuts and bolts, somehow sidestepping Simon and the rest of his security so I can get close enough to dispatch the holy man to actual heaven, where he'll be free to compare his ginned-up version to the real thing.

Seems simple enough.

I have no doubt he'll end up there either. His heavenly reward, I mean. I long ago stopped believing that we're sorted into groups for our eternal retribution, or that there's any door, or pearly gate, that you can't pry open, given enough gold.

I may have once had some thin faith in something like cosmic justice, but now I believe in box-cutters.

Everything else I left buried in a tunnel along with the number 2 train.

25

We'll also need a nurse so I contact Margo.

Margo was my mother's roommate in nursing school, best friend for life after that. When I was a kid she used to sit at our kitchen table, blowing smoke out her nostrils like an angry bull. Nicest woman in the world though. A laugh that could swallow a room. I haven't seen her since my mother passed. My mother didn't last much longer after that incident with the tardy ambulance.

I catch a bus out to the Jersey suburbs, an hour ride to Hackensack. As the city peels away, it feels much saner. Suburban. Almost like life as it was. From the bus you can see into people's lit-up living rooms. The houses out here aren't full of tappers in their silver torpedoes, just people on flowered sofas, planted in front of TVs.

Yes, they still make TV shows somewhere. The rest of the country is still pretty shiny, from what I hear. Apparently the West Coast is more or less the same. Sunshine. Palm trees. Beautiful women in drop-top convertibles. Singing surfers. Moral rot. The whole enchilada, in the shape of California.

I wouldn't know. I've never been. At one time I thought of relocating, right after Times Square. Figured they've got to have garbage out there too.

Very same thought made me stay in the end. A country buried in trash from coast to coast.

As for the rest of it, the in-between part, I hear it's relatively clean and still open for business, like a plucky dollar store. No longer the land of milk and honey, maybe, but at least you can still get high-grade pharmaceuticals on every street corner on the cheap. Most places, they call it the Tooth-less Tap-In. A dream you huff out of a paper bag.

Really, it's just New York that got nuked, cordoned off, shut down, shunned. Capital of the world, cut loose to drift into the sea.

The country's soul, on a funeral pyre.

Margo's in a low-rise. Lots of buildings out here are basically just dorms for support staff, the servant class, who ride in daily to the city to fidget with breathing tubes, feed tubes, shit tubes, piss tubes. Tubes that run in and out like high-ways for all the rush-hour traffic of the human body. Then all the Margos of the world ride the bus back home to catch the day's events on the TV. Or escape the day's events.

Thing about Margo, she's the unhealthiest nurse ever. Chain smokes, obese, has to stop to catch her breath while she's catching her breath.

Then again, as she likes to say, what does health have to do with being a nurse anymore?

She opens a beer for her, then one for me, puts them on the coffee table between us like we're playing chess with only two pieces. I notice there's already several empties stand-ing at attention in the sink. Don't imagine she's had a dinner party lately either.

She follows my eyes to the empties.

So my recycling box is full. What brings you out to Hack-ensack?

Just wanted to check in on you.

That's a funny sentiment to suddenly swell up after eight years.

I'm sorry. I got busy. You know the city.

Really? What are you busy with?

Just the city. It keeps me busy enough.

Well, it's good to see you.

Margo, you ever think of moving closer? Plenty of room in Hoboken. Or Park Avenue, for that matter.

She looks at me like I just asked her if she's ever thought of giving up plumbing and moving right into the sewer.

So I skip to the next question.

How are you keeping? I'm sorry I haven't been out sooner to see you.

Well, if you had come out, I could have told you, I was very sorry to hear about your wife.

Thank you.

We clink longnecks.

She was a beautiful girl. Such a shame. What they did.

I appreciate it.

Shame what happened to this country.

With Margo, you're never far from a tirade. She's not quite the happy snorting bull I remember from my kitchen-table days. She's bigger than ever, but seems deflated. I always figured that one day she'd work her way through every last person in the world to be angry at, and that would leave only her, and then that would be it.

I listen to her for a bit, let her wind down. Then I explain I need to hire a nurse for a job, and she cuts me off.

Does it involve changing a rich man's diapers while he dreams?

No.

She swigs.

Okay then. I'm in.

Margo offers me the couch but I tell her I've got business to get back to in the city. I say goodnight, catch the late-night bus, bound for Port Authority.

Then, a few stops later, hop off.

Plot a detour.

Hoping to clear my head.

So the Crusade is coming in less than a week. It's set to kick off on Sunday night. The mayor has sworn they'll have the camps swept clean by then. Proudly points to news footage of skinny stragglers stumbling out of Central Park, begging for scraps, getting pelted by onlookers, then cuffed and carted away. No one's sure what they're charged with or where they end up. Some rumors say upstate. Some rumors say Fresh Kills. Some rumors say it's best not to listen to rumors, unless you want to find out firsthand.

Second bus unloads me in Hoboken.

Certain times, times like these, I have a few rituals.

Reminders, really.

Of things I need to be reminded of. From time to time.

Not meant for anyone else. Just for me.

Unlock my apartment. Leave the lights out.

Head to the kitchen. Open the icebox.

Stand and stare into the freezer. Where I keep my parceled souvenir.

Actually, reminder's not the right word.

Relic's better.

Freezer's cold curls out, licks my face.

26.

He was a lawyer.

He wasn't the first one.

He was the third.

The first one was an accident. Maybe.

That's what I told myself at the time, anyway.

The first one:

An old trash-duty buddy heard I was in a bad place, bouncing from bed to bar to bed.

This was in the first few months after Times Square.

City still reeling. My apartment still empty. My Stella's clothes still hanging undisturbed in the closet. Waiting in vain to be worn again.

So this old trash-duty buddy tracked me down to this bar I liked on the boardwalk of Coney Island, where the front side opened out to the ocean and the seagulls loitered and chattered like barflies. I'd make the long trip out because I liked to smell the sea.

Smelled sour. Like garbage.

I found that comforting.

He tracked me down and instead of offering condolences, he offered me cash. A dispute had turned ugly and he wanted me to talk to the guy. Just talk. I guess he asked me because I'd recently developed a local reputation as someone who was long past issues of personal concern.

He'd had some argument over money or property or something.

To be honest, I don't remember the details.

I don't even think I knew them back then.

But I was alone and out of work and bed-hopping and burning through what little cash I had left. Rick had cut me a deal and set me up on a discount trip, where I didn't tap into any dream, I just tapped into nothing.

Just a void.

Until my hour was up.

So my old trash buddy sidled up on a barstool and asked me to do him a solid.

Which I did.

Caught the guy outside his apartment one night. Startled him while he searched for his keys.

Big guy. Cocky.

Conversation moved to an alleyway.

He threw the first punch. I'm sure of that.

Or pretty sure.

In any case, it got ugly.

And I still carried my box-cutter.

The one I'd used to slice open that garbage bag.

My reluctant surgeon's tool.

I wasn't nearly so careful on him.

Hands were steadier, though.

So. Problem disappeared. So did the guy.

When you work in garbage, you have access to incineration.

And instead of calling the cops, my friend paid me a bonus. Then lost my phone number for good.

But not before passing it on.

———

That was number one.

The lawyer was number three.

His jilted wife had hired me.

She came to me in a dream.

I was tapped in at Rick's to the darkness, to nothing, and then there she was, like an angel, before me.

Beautiful woman, oddly outlined in light. Face aged by abuse.

Not the kind that comes from belt straps and backhands. That's too downmarket. Too hands-on.

This was just the abuse of pills, neglect, and pain, all etched in her face over time.

She'd bribed Rick to let her slip into my dream.

Then she led me out.

This angel.

We went for bubble tea. Her choice.

Chinatown still bustling back then.

She said she thought her husband was cheating. But not out here.

In there.

That's why she bribed Rick.

She'd never been off-body and she wanted to see what the limnosphere offered him that their life together couldn't match.

To her surprise, in my dream, it offered nothing.

But I assured her that my setup was not typical. Most people prefer some frills and thrills to spice up their oblivion.

Not many people order the abyss, straight up.

She'd lost him, she said. He'd gone in for a business trip but now he was limning ten, fifteen hours a day. He'd left his job, cashed out his securities. She knew he'd met someone in there, some hussy, and now he wouldn't come out.

Hussy.

Her word.

They'd fought. He'd frozen her assets. Forced her to move out. He was tapped in while the moving company carted away her things. The last remnants of their life together. Boxed and bagged like crime-scene evidence.

She said good-bye to him while he lay silently dreaming. Their marriage long dead, now her at his side, mourning it, like an open-casket funeral.

He'd already changed all the passcodes to the bank accounts.

But not to the apartment.

You might recognize him, she said, as we finished our tea, almost as an afterthought.

Why?

He was all over the news for awhile.

Really? For what?

He survived Times Square. Big story. Local news ran wild with it. Front-page of the *Post*, three days running.

I didn't look at the papers after Times Square.

So you don't remember the Lucky Passenger?

When I was a kid, my father was never religious. He saved his Sundays for football and quiet communion at the altar of the couch. No wine, no wafers, just beer and Pringles. He worked hard all week, he said, and if the Lord set Sunday aside as a day of rest, well, who was he to argue with the Lord?

So on Sundays, he rested. And prayed. For the Jets.

My mother's family was more observant. Roman Catholics, many generations back. Her own grandmother was a black-cowled, hunched-over husk of a woman, whispering over her rosary, haunted by the unseen, sputtering curses and prayers. When my mother broke with her family and went to school to be a nurse, not a nun, it broke her grandmother's heart. When I was a kid, my mother never made church a weekly habit. But she did keep her grandmother's rosary hanging from the vanity.

My father she could drag to Mass maybe twice a year. Easter and Christmas. Home in time for kickoff.

But me she was worried about.

Maybe she was right to be.

Either way, for awhile, every week, she'd drop me off for Sunday school. Car pulled to the curb. Hair up in curlers. Lean across the front seat to kiss me on the cheek and promise to pick me up at this exact same spot when Sunday school let out. I could tell her all about what I'd learned.

Figured I'd memorize a few verses. Say a few Hail Marys. Take First Communion. What could it hurt?

None of it stuck, though. And once I got old enough to outgrow my First Communion suit, I found other ways to occupy my Sundays, and my parents didn't complain too loudly.

So I don't remember much of church. A few stories. The odd parable.

The oily smell of incense, swung from the end of a chain.

But there was one thing that left an impression.

Ornate box they kept at the front. By the altar.

Reliquary.

———

It was the easiest thing in the world, like delivering takeout.

The apartment was empty, as advertised, save for him sleeping.

Sensors purring. Monitors cooing.

Fresh feed-bag on an IV.

Not too old, maybe late thirties, well-built guy and as handsome as his wife was pretty. Impeccably suited, down to the silk pocket square that he paid someone to fluff for him each day.

Palatial apartment, tastefully furnished, top floor, panoramic river views.

Realtor's fantasy. Only a wish for most anyone else.

Yet here he was. Lost in the dream.

Framed photos of the happy couple still propped up everywhere as mementoes.

And on the walls, front pages. Framed.

Mounted like trophies.

Post. Daily News. Times. USA Today.

The lawyer, smiling broadly, holding up his right hand. Fingers wide.

Headlines trumpeting.

FORTUNE SPARES THE LUCKY PASSENGER.

The lawyer's name, I learned from the articles, was Charles Pierce.

Come to think of it, I did remember him.

Not from headlines, though. From billboards.

The Lucky Passenger and his famous lucky fingers.

———

The reliquary was treated with a special reverence. Carefully maintained. Never opened, no matter what. Even if you inquired politely for a peek.

So one day I asked my Sunday school teacher what the big deal was.

He looked at me. Got serious.

That box contains the dust of the bones of saints.

What? Like a coffin?

Not exactly. It's a holy place to keep that which has been touched by God. So we may all be inspired. And benefit from its power.

So like souvenirs, I said.

Not souvenirs, he said. Relics.

Charles Pierce had scrambled down the stairs at Wall Street station to catch the uptown 2 train express.

Got snared in the entranceway.

Turnstile jammed.

Swiped his subway card once. Twice. Again.

PLEASE SWIPE AGAIN.

Subway waiting. Doors gaping.

PLEASE SWIPE AGAIN.

PLEASE SWIPE AGAIN.

PLEASE SWIPE AGAIN AT THIS TURNSTILE.

Stupid card keeps—can't get the—doesn't anything work right in this fucking—

Two-tone signal as the subway doors slide shut.

Charles Pierce swiping.

Cursing.

Top of his lungs.

—GODDAMN THIS FUCKING CITY—

Turnstile never budged.

Charles Pierce stands chewing out the bored-looking

booth attendant, finger jabbing the Plexiglas as the uptown express slips from the station.

Red taillights recede into the darkness.

He's still steaming, silently fuming, on the platform when the ground lurches and the tunnel emits a dull bored faraway roar.

THE LUCKY PASSENGER.

All the headlines proclaimed it.

ONE SWIPE FROM DEATH.

Who knows why God chose to spare me, of all people?

Said again and again with a newly sainted shrug.

Repeated in story after story. Quote after quote.

On the couch of the *Today* show.

I honestly can't say why God chose me, Lorelei.

The host nods sympathetically. Recrosses long legs.

He holds up his right hand.

This hand—I was holding the swipe card in this hand—

Chokes up. A well-rehearsed act. Voice hitching on the same word—*special*—every time.

I don't know why God spared me, Lorelei. But I have to believe it's because He has something special in store for me.

Lorelei nods. Her hand on his knee.

Cut to commercial.

He wasn't the only one that day with a story like that, of course.

Lots of people died. Lots didn't.

He's just the one who was smart enough to tell his story to anyone who'd listen. Tell it, then sell it.

First to sell newspapers. Then lotto tickets. Then toothpaste. Then anything he could point at with his famous lucky fucking fingers.

Charles Pierce on a billboard, arms outstretched.

LET'S SEE WHAT BARGAIN MY LUCKY FINGERS HAVE PICKED OUT
FOR YOU TODAY!

After that, her husband was never quite the same, his wife told me over bubble tea. It became clear, with all that attention, her meager devotion was no longer going to be enough. He'd been spared for some higher purpose, he truly believed that. And apparently that higher purpose was selling six-inch submarine sandwiches, among other things.

Half a hoagie grasped in those famous fingers.

Smile to the camera.

Lucky me!

So why should he go back to the normal life? he told her. The one he'd left behind?

But the fame began to drag on him. The constant nagging for handshakes and autographs.

And then he'd started tapping in.

And that's when she'd lost him, she said.

There are three types of relics.

I know. I Googled it.

First order of relic. The physical body of a saint.

Second order of relic. An object the saint once had in his or her possession.

Third order of relic. An object that's come in contact with the first order of relic.

Three orders. Like three outcomes.

And that's it.

The first order, of course, is the holiest. Physical remnants. Which come in many varieties. All with Latin names.

Ex capillus.

Ex ossibus.

Ex cineribus.

Ex pelle.

Ex carne.

From the hair.

From the bones.

From the ashes.

From the skin.

From the flesh.

He lay asleep in an apartment littered with pictures from a life he no longer wanted. Of a wife he had no use for.

A roomful of souvenirs.

Seemed senseless, this flesh-and-blood body just lying there, like a discarded husk.

Body slowly shriveling under a ten-thousand-dollar suit.

He still had everything I'd lost. Everything I'd die to get back.

Yet he still checked out.

Hard not to see it that way, anyway, as I stood there, holding my box-cutter, watching him drift in a dream.

Surrounded by all those photos.

One swipe from death.

And me thinking.

I don't know why God chose you either.

But here we are.

Should have left him there. Left it at that.

Dead lawyer in a bed. Hard to imagine a surplus of questions. Or mourners.

But I didn't.

Instead I carted his body out in a mover's box on a dolly. Wore an old pair of coveralls and a painter's cap tugged low.

Took his body to the usual place. To burn it.

No doubt security cams at his building caught me coming and going. The whole operation sloppy enough that I figured eventually someone would come looking for us both. To be honest, I didn't much worry.

Maybe welcomed it.

Felt the whole world was already spinning the wrong way on its axis.

So let them come for me.

But no one did.

I guess law enforcement had its hands full, what with the city still exploding.

And it turned out there was no one else left in his life to raise a finger in complaint.

Not even a lucky one.

The most holy relic, by the way, is the Eucharist. The communion wafer that's the literal flesh of Christ, transmuted the moment you receive it on your tongue.

Like I told you, I took First Communion.

If you believe in that sort of thing.

Edible flesh.

The holiest ritual.

But don't worry.

I didn't eat the lawyer.

But I did take some souvenirs.

Just four.

Left the thumb.

Box-cutter wouldn't cut it.

So I used a linoleum knife instead.

Curved blade. Have to be careful.

Those things are extra-sharp.

Packed a Ziploc with ice.

Wrapped them up in butcher's paper.

Stashed the whole thing in a duffel bag.

Incinerated the rest of him.

Souvenirs are always a bad idea.

But these aren't souvenirs.

They're relics.

Ex carne.

From the flesh.

Duffel bag dripping on the subway ride home.

When I met his wife again, she paid the back half and thanked me then sat and cried in that same bubble-tea café.

At first I thought she was regretting what she'd done.

Then she told me.

She hadn't been entirely straight with me. She'd known what he was doing in there.

She'd hired someone to tail him into his dream. It's hard to do, but not impossible, if you're technically proficient and ethically flexible. It's one of many services offered by Rick, for example.

So the tail trailed him into his personal construct. The dream he'd built for himself. Abandoned his life for. Abandoned her for.

Came back with a full report.

She'd expected a lavish hotel with some hooker or high-school sweetheart. Or perhaps some more unspeakable depravity. Some secret shameful desire he could never share.

But that wasn't it at all.

It was just their life, exactly re-created. To the last detail.

Same apartment. Same suits. Same view of the city.

Same celebrity endorsements.

All of it identical.

Except without her.

She'd been erased.

So she returned the favor.

I stand in Hoboken. Stare into the icebox.

My reliquary.

Take a moment.

Feel the cold.

When I don't feel it anymore, I close the door.

That's the lesson.

The gospel truth taught to me by my personal patron saint.

No matter what you have, or how lucky you think you are, there's nothing in this world you can hold on to so tightly that it can't be taken from you.

His wife sobbed.

Why would he—

I stopped her.

Took the money.

Stood up.

Explained to her.

I don't care.

And realized only then that it was true.

And that was the last time I listened to a backstory.

Or let anyone pay in installments. Or met with a client face-to-face.

Or laid down in a bed.

Until my meeting with Harrow in the wheat field.

As I left the café that day I stuffed her money into a deep pocket.

Apparently I'd taken to calling them clients now.

27

Rick makes a good living running Rick's Place in China-town, catering to a reliable stream of tappers, but to make extra cash he takes the occasional off-hours private tap-in job, which he scrounges up on the seedy old Internet. Servicing nervous dreamers who want to crash some porny construct they're too embarrassed to ask for by name in the light of day. So Rick's like the kid who opens the back exit to the movie theater, lets you sneak in and sit in the front row for free. Minus his fee, of course. He taps you in, takes his fat envelope, and quietly lets himself out.

Mina is convinced Rick's cheating on her, which he is, so she tries to follow him to these jobs and spy on him, which she can't.

Take tonight.

Rick's on his third house-call when he decides to shake her, which isn't too hard, given that if you stood across the room from her and asked her to walk toward you in a straight line, about half the time she'd get lost on the way.

Compared to that, the back alleys of the Lower East Side are a labyrinth. Rick doubles back a few times, then pops loose, free of his tail, a block from his destination address. He's way south of Rivington, in the crummiest part of a crummy neighborhood. Tired tenements slump by the side-walk, black-iron fire escapes stitched down their bellies like ugly sutures.

He heads into a walk-up with an apartment number on a scrap. Finds the door open so he lets himself in. He has enough time to register that the apartment is dark and entirely bare, save for a wooden rocking chair. But not enough time to turn around before Simon the Magician steps out of the darkness and slashes a sjambok across the back of his knees, which feels to Rick roughly like getting horsewhipped with a live high-voltage wire.

Another nifty trick. Most magicians disappear.

Simon appears.

Rick half-turns and manages to get his hands up this time but that only makes it worse. The sjambok is like a bullwhip that's all handle, no whip, and on the second pass it slices a whistling gash across both of Rick's upheld palms, the skin splitting raggedly, as though gasping in surprise.

Simon then calmly bull-rushes him, sjambok held lengthwise up against his neck and arms, Rick stuttering backward until he slams into drywall.

The cheap wall shudders.

Simon gets to the gun in Rick's belt before Rick does.

Steps backward.

Bounces the pistol lightly in his palm.

It's a snub-nose, for self-protection. Ironic.

Looks like a padlock with a tumor on it.

He waves Rick over to the rocking chair.

Once Rick's hands are bound behind him with plastic cuffs, Simon commences the speech-making.

See, for me? I don't trust guns. Too messy. All forensics and fingerprints. It's much too easy to connect a body to a bullet, and a bullet to a gun, and a gun to a man.

He turns the gun over, studying it, like it's an heirloom.

Not that anyone bothers about that sort of thing anymore, am I right? These days you pop someone in cold blood in broad daylight, FedEx the murder weapon to the cops, it will end up in a folder on a pile somewhere, shrugged off as someone else's problem. But still.

He pockets the pistol.

Old habits. You understand.

He hefts the sjambok.

Now this—

Sends its tip whistling across Rick's face. Tip bites. Halves a tattoo.

—this is more my kind of firepower. They were made to kill snakes. Most are flexible, like a whip. Made of rhino hide, just leather wrapped on leather. This one's custom though—

Bends it. Bounces back to attention. Sounds a metallic twang.

—got a little something extra inside.

Whip whistles back the way it came. Matching slice.

Rick sputters.

Wait—I can—don't you know—just talk to Milgram—

One last slash to shut Rick up.

Sorry. We're long past the let's-make-a-deal phase.

Shakes the sjambok slightly, held upright. Watches it wobble.

Then puts it down.

Retrieves a duffel bag. Pulls out a roll of duct tape. Tears off a piece. Mouth-sized.

As I said, I don't trust guns.

Lays the tape over Rick's mouth. Tape edges grip his cheeks where the cuts are. Tugs them wider.

I'm more of a non-lethal man myself.

Pulls out a penknife. Opens it. Cuts a slit in the tape. Second mouth.

Then he pulls a can of pepper spray from the gym bag. Jumbo-size. For crowd control.

See, this? This you can buy on the Internet. Get it sent to a PO box. No names, ID, nothing. Legal. Untraceable. And non-lethal.

He shakes the can.

For the most part.

Rests the toe of his boot on the chair's rocker. Tilts it forward.

Tips Rick's chin up with the nozzle.

Of course, this is the kind of thing that's used to disperse riots. Entirely safe and more or less harmless when used on large gatherings in the open air. Isn't that what they say?

Simon stoops and pulls a pair of plastic goggles from the duffel bag. Straps them over his eyes.

Then slowly works the nozzle of the pepper-spray can into the slit in the tape over Rick's mouth.

Rick's legs kick, trying to topple the chair backward, but it doesn't topple. Just rocks.

Simon's boot stills the rocker.

But you know what I've discovered?

Works the nozzle further into Rick's mouth.

Best way to make a non-lethal weapon lethal?

One last jam. Rick gags.

Just treat the man like a crowd.

The hissing of the spray goes on long enough that the neighbors assume it's the roach-guy making his regular visit. At least until their own eyes start to water.

When Mina catches up to him, Rick is bent double on the floor, toppled, still bound to the chair, coughing up foamy blood.

Not coughing. Coughed.

She falls and cradles his head until her palms burn. Eyes raw. She coughs, cries.

Simon stands over her.

Gives the empty can one last rattle.

Death rattle.

Then dumps it in the duffel bag.

Stows the goggles too.

Then retrieves a knife that's nasty enough to have no other use than cutting people.

She looks up at him, eyes swollen, welling, and spits.

The fuck are you. Fuck you. I'll fucking kill you.

He stands her up.

His own eyes puffy and raw at the rims, in some parody of mourning.

He smiles.

Don't worry.

She spits again. Not words this time.

He puts his meaty hand behind her head and clutches her skull. Then with his right hand he presses the long blade vertically against the thin skin of her forehead.

She barely squirms.

Rotates the blade counter-clockwise.

Presses again.

Sign of the cross.

Leans in. Whispers.

Go tell them what I've done.

On his way out, duffel bag slung over his shoulder, Simon stops briefly on the street to berate himself, like a man on his way home who forgot to buy milk.

Damn.

I should have asked him what the tattoos meant.

28.

Meanwhile at Trump Tower.

Persephone's alone, reading. A book. *Middlemarch*. Almost done.

Mark's off trawling Chinatown, again, looking for a cheap bed for an hour. Maybe two.

I'm in Hoboken staring into an icebox.

Persephone curls up in the leather chair.

Knock at the door. A voice calls.

Hey. It's Dave the doorman. From downstairs. Got a delivery for Mark Ray.

She puts the book down, perturbed. Calls back.

Sorry. Can't open up for anyone. Doctor's orders.

Come on. It's me, Dave. From downstairs.

No can do, Dave from downstairs.

Seriously, it's me. Take a look in the peephole.

She tips up on tiptoes.

Dave's face all funny. Dave the bug.

Flat-footed again.

Sorry, Dave from downstairs. Can't do it.

He knocks three times on the door with a gun.

Shots echo. Door dimples. Three fresh pimples like a teen before prom.

She calls out.

Dave the dumbass. It's steel-reinforced. Don't you know that?

Knob turns.

Door opens.

Dave invites himself in.

Then I guess I should use the master key, huh?

But she's gone.

He closes the door quietly and locks it behind him. Not a huge apartment, and there's only one way out, unless you plan to rappel.

Pistol pokes its nose into the kitchen. Dave follows.

Still in his Sergeant Pepper's uniform. Brocade at the shoulders.

Epaulets. Captain's hat.

God, he's always hated this thing.

Snaps the kitchen lights on. Empty, and from what he can tell, all knives accounted for in the wooden block.

Silly girl.

Hot, though. Very hot.

She should try wearing something other than sweatpants.

Out to the living room. Picture window hung like a masterpiece.

The sparkling city.

Now, a view like that, he would kill for.

Actually, that's kind of what he's doing right now.

Taps the bathroom door open with the gun snout. Yanks the shower curtain back, *Psycho*-style.

Rings rattle.

Not in there. Not that dumb.

And so into the bedroom.

Appropriate, he thinks.

Convenient too.

———

She knows Dave the doorman. She knows all the doormen by now, of course, but she remembers him in particular, because of the way he looks at her. It's the same look she remembers from certain older men in her congregation. Men in the subway. Boys in the tents. Two men in a van.

From her father, that one night.

She's seen plenty of looks in her life, learned them all, catalogued them, kept mental index cards on all their alarming variety. I want you. I want to love you. I want to fuck you. I want to hurt you.

I want you to know I want to hurt you.

Some people undress you with their eyes. Some people go a lot further than that.

Dave does, often.

So maybe, just maybe, this will work.

Dave the doorman leaves the lights out in the bedroom. Stands framed in the doorway. A square splash of city light falls on the bed, so he spots them.

Bra. Panties. Discarded.

And, from what he can tell, recently worn.

Don't tell me I caught her in the middle of a shower.

Better yet. Bubble bath.

He steps in gingerly, makes the here-kitty-kitty noise, like in a movie. Not too many more places left where she could be. Maybe the closet.

Maybe she's in the closet watching him right now.

He prods the panties with the gun muzzle.

Scoops them up.

Retrieves them from the end of the pistol, like a fresh-caught fish on a hook.

Balls them up.

Inhales them.

A perfumer's inhale.

Eyes slip closed for a second.

Her hand joins his from behind, her body up against his, breasts pooled against his back, and he almost thinks, for a second, that he conjured her. Her hand is clutching his hand that's clutching the panties and now she's pushing them into his mouth. Panty taste.

Her other hand takes its best educated guess at where his kidney is and slides the knife in, searching.

Twists it twice, a full rotation. Like working on a stubborn screw.

To leave a more raggedy wound.

He struggles to shrug her off but she's already disarming him. Funny what you can pick up after a few weeks living in tents.

Gun falls softly to the plush carpet.

He follows. Less softly.

She straddles him. Improvises on his neck with the blade.

She's not a medical student, after all. But more or less anything that's there to be cut, she cuts.

The plush soaks up most of what pumps out.

She has discovered a streak inside herself of late that she does not recognize. She tries to credit it to carrying the baby. If credit is the word.

Something instinctual, born of being a mother. Some new primal drive to protect.

Though that doesn't quite explain it.

Those two guys in Red Hook, for example. She lingered long after she should have left them.

Working. Slowly.

And now here.

Dave the doorman. In his sad little epaulets.

She wonders where it comes from. Or if it was always there.

Latent.

Maybe her father saw it in her all along.

He kept a claw-foot tub in the basement for one purpose. Called it the Baptismal.

Bare lightbulb jumped when he yanked the chain. Black shadows danced like a campfire.

Started back before she could remember, really. Became a weekly ritual. Saturday nights. Her mother standing silent as he marched her down the stairs.

Faucet roared, openmouthed, until the tub filled to the top.

Then the timid mouse-squeak as he twisted the spigot shut.

Last drop trembling on the mouth of the faucet.

Drip.

He made her strip down. Kneel naked on a stepstool. Curl over. So he could dunk her head underwater.

One. Two. Three.

Pull her up.

One. Two. Three.

Pull her up.

All the while reciting scripture.

Her long hair, her mother's pride, never cut, left a wet slash on the wide wooden boards of the wall as he yanked her up quickly.

Then dunked her.

One. Two. Three.

Four. Five.

If she'd been especially bad.

Then he handed back her flannel nightie, folded neatly. Freshly laundered.

Told her, Now you are clean.

Her mother never once mentioned it.

Not once, and then she died.

The weekly ritual. She almost came to—what? Not enjoy it exactly. But rely on it? Maybe that's it. This weekly cleansing.

The comforting consistency of rules.

It let her know that, whatever she did, she could be exonerated.

Washed clean.

Through this weekly reminder of her father's unwavering love.

Though as a teenager, she started to feel rightly more ashamed to remove her nightgown.

And her father had to find a sturdier stepstool.

Still. Nothing happened. Not of that sort.

Maybe to Rachel.

But not to her.

Not to her.

Until he saw those pictures.

He exploded into her bedroom wielding the glowing tablet.

The light from the tablet lit his furious face.

Slapped her with a bony backhand.

First time he'd ever hit her.

Drew blood. Just a trickle though.

Then he marched her downstairs.

She accepted it meekly.

Stripped. Knelt. Prayed.

As he held her under.

One. Two. Three.

Four. Five.

Six. Seven.

Eight.

Nine.

Long enough for her to worry this was more than punishment.

Still under.

Every muscle tensed.

Tendrils of blood curled and sniffed around her face like a school of curious fish.

She gasped and breathed water.

She had to breathe something.

He pulled her up.

She spat and sputtered and tasted something salty and metallic and then he pushed her under again.

One. Two. Five. Eleven. Nineteen.

She lost count.

The frigid water set her ears to ringing.

She was curled over, on her knees, naked.

With one hand he held her head under.

His other hand went wandering.

Sounds of the room muted.

He was saying something. Not scripture.

Her eyes open underwater.

Sick.

Feeling a fullness.
Edges of her sight blacking out—
—like a curtain falling.
He pulled her up.
Fingers still in her.

The next time under she just let go.
Stopped struggling. Started to float.
Loosed her breath in a school of lazy bubbles.
Perhaps she'd always deserved this.
One last bubble, like a hiccup.
The room so faraway and quiet.
Calming.

She only felt a joyful sinking.

Fringed in black.
Black bubbles. Arriving to carry her upwards.
To whatever reward awaited her.

Then a last rude yanking and a gasp and one last watery slash painted on the wide-plank wall, crude calligraphy left by the wet brush of her long hair, never cut, her mother's pride.

And now here.
Dave the doorman. In his sad little epaulets.
Painting his own wet slashes.
He long ago stopped spasming.
Yet these dirty fucking panties still won't fit all the way in his mouth.
So she cuts him a wider smile.

That's better.

Something about becoming a mother, she tells herself. That's what she likes to think.

Mother's pride.

Then she likes to stop thinking, and that helps, for awhile.

29

By the time I get back to Mark Ray's apartment, there is a body, and a wet swamp of blood, and Mark's there, and he is crying.

I'm sorry. I should have been here. I'm sorry.

Hands me the note.

A kid's scrawl. Thumbprints in blood like lipstick kisses in the margins.

You said you would protect me.

Persephone's gone.

We lock the front door behind us and figure we've got at least three days until someone reports the stink.

Speaking of three days and stink, Harrow's Crusade is rolling into town.

In three days.

Ready or not.

Back in Hoboken, I read about Rick in the *Post*.

Body in a dumpster.

Tattoos closed the case.

GANGLAND SPRAY SLAY.

The *Post* really needs to find a new synonym.

Mark Ray doesn't drink, doesn't smoke, doesn't curse, but right now, on my sofa, he's drinking, smoking, and cursing.

The smoking's not going so well. He gets through two puffs. Rick's brand. In memoriam.

These are fucking gross.

Stubs it out.

Pardon my language.

Swigs a beer. Holds it up to the light.

So people throw away their whole lives just for this?

It's an acquired taste.

Mark puts the bottle down.

Okay. What now, mastermind?

You're the mastermind, Mark. I'm the muscle.

Well, we have to find her. That's first.

Is it? What for? We haven't exactly done a bang-up job on her behalf so far.

Are you kidding? You saved her.

The only person I really saved her from so far is me. Everyone else, not so much.

Mark stands up. Paces. Hard to imagine how he ever lies still in a bed. He turns to me.

So what then? That's it?

No. Like you said. Three true outcomes.

Okay. Well. Giving her to them is not an option anymore. Not that it was.

No, it wasn't.

So that's out. And without her, we have no prayer of luring Harrow into the dream. Which is fine, because without Rick, we have no prayer of crashing their construct in any case. Unless you know of someone else who you trust who can pull that kind of thing off.

Not offhand.

So that part's out. Which also means I'm more or less useless to you now, because if it comes down to a street fight out here, in the nuts and bolts, realistically, you're on your own.

Seems so.

And I don't know what you may have in mind, but I can't see a way for you to pull this off cleanly by yourself.

Me neither.

So there you go. There aren't three outcomes anymore, Spademan. Only two. Maybe not even two. Just one.

Which is?

He kills you. He kills her. He kills us all.

That's a terrible outcome.

No kidding.

Mark slumps back on the leather sofa. Knees bobbing. Can't sit still. I can tell he wants badly to puzzle this out. I can also tell he can barely wait to tap back in and be rid of this puzzling world. But he won't abandon me. I like him for that. He also doesn't have his answer yet.

But I do. So I tell him.

You're wrong, Mark. There are still three outcomes.

Really? Are you planning on sharing them with me?

Yes. Three outcomes. He kills me. I kill him. Or both.

Mark stares me down. Silent for a moment. Then scoffs.

Sure. Back to the kamikaze plan. Brilliant.

You said yourself, no way we get close enough to Harrow out here and still get out alive.

Yes, but you're missing the most important part of that statement, which is the getting-out-alive part.

You and I both know she's out there right now, running. Alone. Thanks to us. Thanks to me. And Harrow won't stop until he finds her, Mark. You know that. Which he will.

Spademan, stop it. It's suicide.

I shrug.

You have a better idea?
Come on. It's not an option.
It was for you.

Here's the part I can't explain to Mark.
It's been a long time since I needed to do something.
I've done a lot of things, but not out of need.
And I've learned there are a lot of ways, and ugly places,
where things can end.
Backyards. Garbage bags. Subway trains.
Most people don't get to choose.

We don't discuss it further. Watch football instead.
While Mark works on acquiring a taste for beer.
Overtime. Fumble.
Miami scores.
I flip the channel.
Fucking Jets.

Another note.
This one hand-delivered.
Slides under the door like a base-runner stealing home.
By the time I get the door open, hallway's empty.
They just want us to know that they know.

Note's from Milgram.
I believe I mentioned we'd be getting back in touch.

30

Milgram meets me the next day at dawn at the Hoboken waterfront in a stretch limo. Morning air is just cold enough
that you can barely see your breath. The sun's rising across
the river, over the city, peeking through the curtain of towers
like a shy actress on opening night.

Lights come up.

A farmboy, this one in khakis and a button-down, frisks
me with impressive inventiveness. Makes certain not a
square inch goes unfondled. Finds a few hollows I'd forgot-
ten existed.

This Harrow fellow. Real hands-on operation. At all levels.

Farmboy pockets the box-cutter he finds hidden in my
boot. Left there more as a test than anything else.

Milgram dismisses the muscle.

Just the two of us in the backseat.

He knocks twice on the dark glass.

We drive.

Milgram gestures at Manhattan.

It's a bit of a cliché, I know, this meeting in the limo. But
it's quiet, it's private, and it's a great way to see the city.

The skyline passes. Actually, it doesn't pass. We pass.

Amazing, isn't it? After all that's happened? The city still
has a grandeur, don't you think?

I tend to favor this side of the river.

Well, why not? Over there, they have to look at sunset over

New Jersey. You get to watch the sun rise over New York. Pastor Harrow doesn't understand the allure of this city, frankly. Sees it as a cesspool, a kind of new Sodom. But I get it, though. I do. New York. The greatest concentration of human potential in the history of the world. So much so that they had to start piling the people one on top of the other. An island so crowded it had nowhere to go but up.

Yeah, well, it's not so crowded anymore.

I'm amazed you stayed, all these years. After what happened. So many people vacated.

Not all.

No. But most. And many of those who stayed simply dropped out of life, holed up in their metallic cocoons. Well—look at this woman. That's curious.

A jogger huffs up the waterfront, trailing steam clouds, like a locomotive. I'll admit, it's a strange sight. I haven't seen a jogger in years.

Now that's hopeful, isn't it? People out again. Out in their bodies again. That's what our crusade is all about, Mr Spademan. New York. Reborn.

I understand you have some other business in the city while you're here.

He forges on. A salesman. Knows when to engage. When to ignore.

It's an enticing idea, isn't it? Rebirth. Especially for a man like yourself. What you went through. I would think—well, you know. Memories. Regrets. They can form a toxic cloud of their own. A different kind of fallout, I imagine.

Milgram's dressed in a navy suit. Red tie. Perfect knot. A politician's uniform. He flicks at his lapel, brushing away some blemish only he can see. Wears a lapel pin. A tiny silver cross. Readjusts it. Turns back to me.

You must wonder from time to time. What if someone's

wife had missed her train? Or what if her teacher had called in sick and the acting class was cancelled? Or—and these are just hypotheticals, mind you—what if her husband calls her back for one more good-bye kiss in the doorway of their apartment? So she sets off five minutes later. These troubling questions of timing—

Milgram, I'm going to cut you off right there—

I just mean it can all feel so random, so meaningless. That's all we try to do, Mr Spademan. Bring meaning to people's lives. Order.

Persephone told me what you like to do. For example, to her friend.

Rachel? Yes. A troubled girl.

Milgram looks away, out the window, like a shy little boy caught in a lie.

I like to believe she's in a better place now.

I'm sure you like to believe that. Let me interrupt the sales pitch, Milgram. You, me, Harrow, we're all of us a little bit sick. Some of us sicker than others. And I don't see a way that any of us are getting out of this alive.

Well, that's a very dark view of the world.

Not dark. Just a view.

Well, let me offer you an alternate view. We have asked something of you. To give us someone. We've made an offer in return, and it's a good offer, and that offer stands. But let me add one more thing.

I don't need a sweetener.

Hear me out. We have something else we can offer to you. Someone, actually.

Like I said—

Do you recall how many people were involved in the attacks that day?

I never read the papers.

There were six. That they know of. That they caught or were killed. The two in the van. The two they caught in Brooklyn who helped build the bombs. The one who supposedly left the first bag on the train. And the money man. The elderly one. So that's six. The Dirty Half-Dozen, as they dubbed them.

Sure.

And then of course whoever coordinated those car bombs that came after.

They never proved those were related.

All chaos is related, don't you think? In any case. Our Dirty Half-Dozen. The Times Square bombers. Do you know what always fascinated me about their plan?

What?

The precision of it. I mean, you really have to marvel. A subway bomb, then a second one, precisely timed, and then a van that drives down to Times Square all the way from up-state.

Sure. Very impressive. Gold star.

But do you truly believe that, in an operation that well-executed, that precise, you'd leave a bag to ride unattended on a train for—what? Half an hour? From borough to borough? Hoping no one spots it? No one gets suspicious? No one sees something, says something, as they used to say?

I don't really care about logistics. Especially in hindsight.

They say the bag with the bomb on the train rode in alone all the way from Brooklyn. Just like your wife, Mr Spademan.

Your point?

There was a seventh man.

That's bullshit.

A motorman.

That's not true.

He worked for the MTA. Begged off his shift at the station right before the explosion. A half hour earlier than scheduled. Called ahead. Claimed to be nauseous.

So?

So there is one place you could leave a bag and no one would notice. Right at the front of the train. The motorman's car.

Sure. But who would—

You leave the bag, radio ahead, complain that you're ill. Replacement driver meets you, takes over, spots the bag, figures you left it, figures he'll drop it off for you at the next stop. But there was no next stop.

If that's true, if it's even half-true, how come no one knows about it? How come the police never tracked this guy down? They put every fucking speck of every person from that day under a magnifying glass. Trust me.

I don't know. What I do know, Mr Spademan, is that this motorman is out there. And no one's asked him these questions yet.

He puts a hand on my arm. Pale as soap. Perfect manicure.

We thought you might be interested in asking him yourself.

Okay, Milgram. But why tell me now? Why not before?

For most men, the promise of the dream is enough. More than enough. They'll happily make that bargain.

Milgram works past his habitual wince to an actual smile.

We understand that you're different. Persistent. And ruthless. I must say, I thought we had you cornered. But what you did to the Chinaman? I almost admire it. I'm not even sure how you knew he'd turned.

You mean Rick? You fuckers killed him. Sent your errand boy Simon.

Milgram squints, as though I've just told him a joke he doesn't understand. Then continues.

In any case, Mr Spademan, here is our proposal. You give her to us, we give him to you. I will drop you on his doorstep personally. Hand-delivered. Give you two a little privacy. Maybe you get to put that box-cutter to use after all.

Milgram's presentation is over. He's clearly pleased with himself. Folds his pearly hands in his lap. Leaves me to ponder. We ride in silence while I consider what he's told me. No real reason to trust him, but then, this is too big a lie to be a lie. He'd never dangle this if he couldn't deliver. Consequences would be far too grave.

A seventh man. Out there. Unpunished.

There's no way I'll ever give Milgram anything he wants. But I'll admit it. I feel it. Temptation, I mean. Years ago, Mark Ray asked me if I'd ever been tempted by religion, and I told him that's not the kind of temptation I have to worry about.

The limo's circled back to my block. Milgram drops me at my door. A considerate date.

I get out.

Let me think about it.

He leans across the expanse of black leather.

Please do. Pastor Harrow's in the city this weekend, as you know. He'd be happy to meet with you. In person this time. Assuming we can work something out. You have my card. Until then.

The limo drives off. I turn to head home.

On my doorstep, my box-cutter. The one they confiscated. Red ribbon tied around it, like a gift.

31

I'm sitting with Mark Ray on the front steps of the library. Watching the lions watch the city.

This is the first day we met.

He's finishing his story. The one about temptation.

Mark had two friends. Beth and David.

Beth he'd known since middle school. David since diapers.

They grew up in the church together. Sunday school. Youth choir. Easter pageant. Wednesday-night volleyball, followed by prayer.

In their teens, Beth and David started dating. It seemed natural enough. Beth had blossomed into the belle of the congregation. Brunette. Hourglass. David plenty handsome too. Sandy-haired and smiling. They swapped chastity vows and promise rings.

Perfect couple. A billboard for God's good bounty, bestowed on those He loves. On those who obey. They looked like Adam and Eve strolling Eden, pre-serpent.

Everyone said so.

Save Mark.

He couldn't help himself.

He was gripped with lust.

———

He hoped Bible school would quell it. He got accepted to all of them, and chose the one farthest away.

At Bible school he walked the ring road on campus with other women, in among the chastely courting couples.

On your third walk around the ring road, you were allowed to hold hands.

Still, at night, alone, the lust found him.

Gripped him.

He lay in bed after lights-out. Gripped himself.

Then stopped himself.

Prayed instead.

For some kind of release.

He heard on Facebook that David and Beth had split up. Saw Beth's status changed to single.

Started waking up joyful for the first time in months.

Put in for a job at his old church. Youth pastor.

The Prodigal returns. A fisher of men.

His first day back, unpacking books in his new office, Beth and David stopped in to surprise him with a welcome-home basket. Warm socks and hot cocoa. His favorite treat, or so she remembered. He used to clutch hot cups of cocoa on the sidelines when the youth group went ice-skating at the pond. Watching the two of them skate in lazy circles, oblivious to anyone else.

She didn't know it had just been something to hold on to. An excuse to sit it out. Hot cocoa, slowly going cold. He always poured it out into a snowbank when it was time to head home.

They handed him the basket.

Standing hand in hand.

Welcome back.

He smiled.

We patched things up.

He smiled wider.

Great news.

A smile he'd practiced for years and would eventually perfect.

He worked with the teens, the youth. Went from Wednesday-night volleyball star to referee. Whistle at his lips. Later led the prayers.

All the girls formed crushes, naturally. Ray of Sunshine, they called him. Ray of Light. Told him he looked like that guy from the old TV show. *The Greatest American Hero.*

I'm no hero, he told them, American or otherwise.

The older girls liked to sneak up behind him, finger his curls playfully and in mock wonder, until he brushed them off like horseflies, told them to cut it out. They also liked to linger a little too long in the passenger seat of the car when he gave them rides home. Engine idling. Pregnant moment.

Nothing happened.

He was pure. An excellent pastor.

He'd drop them off and drive home alone. Stay up late reading in the lamplight. But it always found him.

Home, at school, back home, it didn't matter.

Gripped with lust.

He turned out the lamp.

One day Beth and David stopped back at his office.

Hand in hand.

Good news. We got engaged.

Later, alone, David asked Mark to be the best man.

He said he'd be honored, of course.

I wouldn't think of asking anyone else.

You're a lucky man. She's a catch.

A year later they stopped by his office again.

He looked up from his lesson plan. The story of Bath-sheba.

What now? Pregnant?

No smiles. Beth's eyes red.

We need to ask your advice.

By all means. Have a seat.

David was considering a missions trip to Mexico.

Mark grimaced. The only news from that region was of drug tensions and body counts. Both rising.

Not the safest spot on the globe.

David nods.

You go where you're called to go.

Beth speaks up.

We're also talking about starting a family.

I see.

David shrugs.

But that means if I'm ever going to go on a missions trip, the time is now. And it's only a year.

She swats him.

Only?

Smiling. But nervous. Sick over this.

She's grown into such a beautiful woman.

Mark clicks his pen.

Recalls school. The nights, mostly.

Clicks the pen again. Clickety-click.

Embossed on the side of the pen: the cross.

The old rugged cross.

Clickety-click.

Puts the pen down.

Looks David square in the eye.

Best friends since childhood.

Go.

Mark leaned forward. Elbows on knees. Hands gripped to whiteness.

Watching the lions. Watching New York. Where he wound up.

Confessing to a stranger on cold stone steps.

David never even made it to the guesthouse. The flight hit bad weather, got delayed, arrived past dark. They decided to risk it, which was stupid, of course. The stubborn gumption of the faithful, as my grandfather liked to say. Hit a road block. No doubt he tried to convert them, even to the end.

I'm sorry.

It's not a story about temptation at all. Don't you see? Not about lust, or love, but punishment. God's wrath. How it follows you. When the Lord is displeased.

He rubbed his hands like he was trying, and failing, to get warm.

Said it like something he'd only just remembered.

But the thing David had done displeased the Lord.

Sounds to me like you're mostly punishing yourself.

Look at me. Playing shrink.

Well, if that's true, I'm doing a terrible job. That's why I called you. Failed even at that.

So what happened with her?

Beth? She was crushed, of course. Broken, really. Inconsolable.

You didn't try? To comfort her?

No. I couldn't even look at her. Not after that. So I ran.

But you loved her.

He looked at me.

Not her. Him.

32

I pull off the red ribbon, pocket the box-cutter, but don't head inside. Not yet.

There's a place in Hoboken where I like to go to when I need a moment to think. The door says SOCIAL CLUB, but really it's just a bunch of old guys playing cards who know how to make you feel unwelcome. My first visit, they shunned me like they were Amish farmers and I was selling electric razors door-to-door. By visit three, I was getting good at shooting my own withering looks at any hapless strays who happened to stumble in. It's the kind of place where an espresso appears at your elbow without asking and fistfights break out over checkers. Just try opening up a chess board, you'll get cuffed upside your brainiac noodle.

So after Milgram drops me off, I decide to make a detour.

Sit a bit and think about that motorman.

Espresso appears. Without asking.

I nod a thank-you to the waiter.

He nods back.

Puts down a second cup.

I've never told anyone about this place, not Mark, not Rick, not anyone, so imagine my surprise when Simon the Magician pulls out the chair opposite mine.

Chair legs scrape the tile floor with a squeal.

Canasta players frown.

Simon the Magician.

Ta-da.

He sits down, folds his hands in front of him, and sighs, like he's come to break up with me. Then he opens his hands.

You want to go somewhere, get something to eat? Maybe pancakes?

I'm more of a waffle man.

Of course. Well then, let me cut right to it. I know you just met with Milgram. I know what he offered you.

Okay.

Let me offer something better.

I'm all ears.

You keep the girl. I give you Harrow.

I lean in, so as to not be overheard.

To be truthful, given what you did to my friend, I'm inclined to just come across this table right now and cut your face and keep cutting until I hit something hard.

He scratches at his beard.

Ah yes. Your friend. Ugly but necessary.

Really? Why's that?

He gestures between us, like now we're connected.

You have him, you don't need me. Now you need me.

Maybe we should continue this discussion outside.

We can do that, sure. But we tried that once and I don't remember it ending too well for you.

That was a dream. This is the nuts-and-bolts world. I do better out here.

Simon watches me. His fingertips drumroll the tabletop.

Spademan, let me invite you to take the long view for once. Your gizmo buddy is dead. Respiratory issues.

Don't be cute.

In any case. He's gone on to his earthly reward. Without

him, your whole plan falls apart. You still want Harrow, but you know you won't get within fifty yards of him with anything like a weapon in your hand. And he still wants the girl, and he still has me, and I'm still very good at my job.

He pauses, rubs his palms together, like he's considering whether or not to betray a confidence. Then he leans in. Voice low.

But this is where I can help you. Or I can get up right now and disappear from your life. At least temporarily. Your call.

Leans back. Having finished his pitch.

I shrug.

Truth is, Simon, you're too late. She already bolted. Right after you sent one of your cronies to kill her.

My crony?

Sure. Turncoat doorman. He's uptown right now, doing the backstroke in his own blood. Her work, not mine.

Simon grins.

Backstroke, huh?

Maybe more of a dead man's float.

Simon pats his pockets. While he does this he says:

But I thought you were supposed to protect her, Spademan.

Yeah, well, so did she.

He pulls a cellphone from his pocket.

Lucky for you, I can help you with that too.

Tosses the phone on the table. Phone spins like spin-the-bottle. Stops at me.

I watch him. He seems like that rare, enviable man completely content in the world. I feel an angry urge welling up to toss the table aside, I could be on him in a second, I'd have a moment or two to leave a permanent mark before he recovered. After that, it would just be animal time, two dumb beasts clawing. No one here would say a word, let alone intervene. These old men have seen worse and kept silent. That's how they all lived to be so old.

But then I think of Mark and temptation. *The sword devours one as well as another.*

Then I think of Persephone.

And I ask what I shouldn't ask.

So what will it cost?

Simon's grin upgraded to a smile.

What does anything cost?

He names his price and just like that, we're just two merchants haggling, over spices, over fabrics, over slaves, a scene as old as the world.

I have a nest egg. His price isn't the whole thing, but close enough.

I have to ask him one more thing, though.

What about the motorman?

He pauses. Considers.

What about him?

For starters, does he exist?

Sure. Best as I know.

Where do I find him?

Simon looks me over. Wonders if this is a deal-breaker. I wonder the same thing.

Settle down, chief. One deal at a time.

I want a name, Simon.

Forget that. This isn't about that. This is about this.

And if there is a time to leave, draw a line, take a stand, this is it. I don't. Instead I say:

How do I know I can trust you?

He holds his hands out.

Nothing up my sleeve.

What you did. I don't forgive you.

I don't expect that you would.

Last question. Why?

You familiar with the term simony?

No. I do know Judas, though.

He sips his coffee.

Well, then, you get the drift.

Black Judas.

Says to me:

Do you remember that old game show where they put someone in a plastic booth, turn the fans on, and dollar bills start swirling? You had to grab all the money you could?

Sure.

I always thought that would be a much more interesting game if they put two people in the booth. Let them fight it out.

He backs his chair up.

More like life.

He stands.

Also, Harrow is old. And his empire is vast. And, like nature, I also abhor a vacuum.

He reaches out his hand. No more wrecking ball of bone. Just a hand.

I want to say deal with the devil, and it is, but that's not all it is.

Dumb luck.

Sometimes you have to hope it comes when you need it.

We shake.

Okay, Simon. Now how do I find her?

Simon points to the phone.

First number on speed-dial.

And why on earth do you think Persephone would answer a phone call from you?

Trust me. She'll pick up.

33

This time, she finds me.

I get back to my apartment and she's already there wait-ing, dressed in her hoodie, Docs laced over sweatpants, like a soldier.

Chatting with Mark.

Seems happy to see me.

Hey.

Hey. You came back.

Yep. And I brought friends.

Eight mangy stragglers, refugees from the camps. Hard to tell the boys from the girls. Too much grime and everyone's got dreadlocks.

I hate dreadlocks.

I spot the one guy with the sliced-up forehead. I guess he and Persephone patched things up.

They're all hungry, too, siege-starved, haven't eaten in a week. Spent the last of their energy dodging nightsticks and paddy wagons. Tossed every trash can they passed for food on their way here, found nothing.

There aren't a lot of pedestrians in the city anymore. So no trash.

No real use for garbagemen.

I order a tower of pizzas from the one place in Hoboken that still delivers. Hurricanes, blackouts, bombs spewing toxic waste, you call their number, they never don't answer. I like that.

Fresh and hot in twenty minutes.

Plus, the name of the joint is the Last Slice.

I like that too.

My kind of place.

While we're waiting, one hungry kid wanders off and starts rooting through my barren fridge. Finds nothing but bottled water and waffle batter.

So he opens the freezer.

Just a Ziploc.

Takes it out. Shakes it. Thinks maybe he's found my secret stash.

Which he has, sort of.

Gropes the baggie. Squeezes the paper-wrapped package. Feels four stiff cylinders.

Smiles.

Dude. This is some serious spliffage.

I take the Ziploc from him. Politely. Place it back inside the freezer.

Trust me. It's too much for you.

Bummer.

Close the freezer door sharply while his hand still lingers on the opening.

He snatches his hand away.

I give him a smile of my own.

Tell him.

Watch your fingers.

Eighteen minutes later. Doorbell.

Pizza's here.

———

They have a kind of party, finish off the last of Mark's beer.

I sit with Persephone.

I was worried.

I'm okay.

Don't run away.

Don't leave me alone.

Fair enough.

We sit a minute more, wait for the city to make the next sound.

Then she says:

So you met Simon.

In the flesh.

And he'll help us?

We'll see.

She reaches out, rubs my arm.

I heard about Rick. I'm sorry.

Thank you.

If he's out, does that mean we're screwed?

Maybe. Maybe not. I may have found us a replacement.

Okay. So what's next?

Honestly, that's between me and your father.

She pulls her hand back.

Not exactly. I had a day to think about it. Which I did.

And?

And I have an idea.

Good. Me too.

She looks at me. All business.

I'm pretty sure you'll like my idea better.

———

Mark and Persephone escort the gang of carcasses out for a field trip to the riverfront. Fresh air. Sunshine. I tell Mark to maybe throw a few in, for a bath.

Truth be told, I'd asked for privacy. Miracle of miracles, I got it.

I finger the business card.

Then call Milgram.

She wants to talk to him first. Alone.

Naturally.

Not here. In there.

Why?

She's scared. Understandably. This way is more comfortable for her. She needs to clear the air.

We can arrange that. Not a problem.

And I want to meet with him. In person. To hand her over.

Of course.

And I want the motorman.

He will be delivered to you. After you deliver her to us. Understood?

Yes. I'll deliver her.

I hang up. Turn to Mina.

White cross of bandage on her forehead.

Red cross, etched in blood, seeping through.

Black cross, underneath, stitched in sutures.

You sure you can do this?

Look. I was his girl, not his fucking apprentice. But I do know my way around a bed. And I am plenty fucking motivated, I will tell you that.

I hope so.

If I wasn't, would I have tracked your ass all the way here?
To fucking New Jersey?

Skinny Mina. Mina saves the day. Maybe.

Mina Machina.

34

Sunday.

New York Reborn.

Madison Square Garden jammed to the rafters, if it still had rafters anymore.

A gospel choir kicks it off. A thunderstorm of tambourines. Across the stadium, fifty thousand hands clap in unison.

Then a warm-up sermon. Opening slot. Light the fire, stoke the brimstone. Local preacher, made good.

Then T. K. Harrow appears.

Angelic. Faintly glowing.

Waves left. Waves right.

Hosannas rain down.

His image wobbles a little, then corrects.

He smiles.

Hologram.

Most know. Few care.

All cheer.

I'm down in the financial district, back at that same abandoned bank. Hike the stone steps and enter. My footfalls echo in the lobby. Farmboy heads me off at the pass.

Farmboy is just as good at frisking as I remember. Finds the box-cutter in my boot and a pistol besides.

My gun. I finally dug it up.

He confiscates both.

Ushers me in.

In Chinatown, Mina in darkness hovers over two beds. Mark in one, Persephone in the other, side by side, like a blood transfusion about to begin.

Tubes and wires strung in between. Mina lit by the blue glow of her laptop. Whole thing rigged like she's trying to jumpstart a car that's been dead for a century.

Margo the nurse sits behind her, smoking.

You sure you can do this?

Mina, cranky.

You worry about the vital signs. This part I got.

Mark and Persephone already gone into the limnosphere. Eyeballs shiver under closed lids. Off to see the wizard.

Mina, crankier.

This chick is pregnant, you know.

I know.

So you shouldn't smoke.

Margo blows fumes out her nose like a bull about to charge.

Don't worry. It's okay. I'm a nurse.

In the dream.

Persephone, alone.

Barefoot.

She's dressed in her baptismal dress. Father's favorite. Floral pattern. Matches the pastures that stretch out on either side of the path before her.

The cobblestones cool underfoot.

Radiant.

Catch the sun and amplify it back at her.

She squints.

Wow, he wasn't kidding.

Paved with gold.

Milgram greets me with a handshake like I'm here to apply for a loan.

His smile tells me I'm not going to get it.

Mr Harrow will be with us shortly. He's just finishing up his meeting. With her. Hopefully all will go well.

No worries. I can wait. Between here, heaven, and Madison Square Garden, Mr Harrow is a busy man today.

The frisking farmboy is joined by three more farmboys. Muscles bulge under shirts. Guns bulge under jackets. They form a loose semicircle around me and Milgram, like he's the cowboy and I'm a skittish calf that might bolt. The frisking farmboy hovers directly behind me like he's daydreaming of all the different parts of me he could break, once he's given the go-ahead.

Milgram folds his arms.

And they say you can't be everywhere at once.

I shrug.

Miracles of the modern world.

Milgram nods.

Indeed.

Margo, still smoking. Having cracked pack number two.

That cut on your forehead looks nasty. You get that looked at?

It's fine.

Mina stroking, then coaxing, then cursing her keyboard. Mutters.

Now where did you get to?

What happened?

Seriously, I need quiet right now.

Long suck on a cigarette. Paper sizzles.

You didn't lose her, did you? Somewhere in there?

No.

No?

No. I didn't.

Okay, good.

Mina scours the screen.

Not her. Him.

She follows the path through the pasture. Butterflies flutter and land on her softly.

The path ends at a temple.

End of the yellow brick road.

The temple is columned, like in Roman times. Or someone's idea of Roman times.

She climbs the stairs to the towering oaken doors.

Each one as tall as a building in its own right. Round iron knockers, big as hula hoops, for giants, she guesses.

The rest of the temple made of gold.

Two farmboys, strapping lads, stand sentry. Dressed as centurions. They stay silent.

The doors swing open.

Inside, a courtyard.

Statues.

Fountains.

At the far end, a throne.

Her father stands.

Milgram kills time by giving me a tour, like we're in a museum.

At one time, banks were thought of almost like churches. I mean, look at this structure. It's magnificent. The painting on the ceiling alone would have taken months to complete. And the vault. Breathtaking, no? A kind of holy of holies in its own right. It's sad to think it's all moved online now. Data zipping hither and yon. All so ephemeral. Nothing left to stain your fingers with.

While he prattles I think of what Persephone told me. About the dream. About Paved With Gold.

About Rachel.

Milgram was the mastermind.

You look beautiful, Grace.

Her father, in a rippling white robe. Majestic. Imperial. Laurel wreath on his brow. His obsession with emperors. He can name the succession by heart. Augustus. Tiberius. Caligula. Claudius.

So much for the footsteps of the humble carpenter, huh, Dad?

I know it's all a bit over-the-top, Grace. But you know, render unto Caesar and so on. And don't forget, this is heaven. Or as close as most people will ever get. And when we all get to heaven, we do want it to look a little bit like heaven.

He descends the few stairs that lead down from the throne.

I was so worried about you.

Really?

Don't ever run away from me again.

I didn't think I was safe with you.

Well, we have a mutual interest in your safety now, don't we?

He reaches out to touch her belly.

She bats his hand away. Maternal instinct.

He smiles.

Why do I have to learn about these things from other people, Grace? It leads to all sorts of misunderstandings. But you should have known I'd never let a grandchild of mine come to harm. Whatever his provenance.

He reaches out. Grazes her cheek with a knuckle.

She flinches. Can't help it.

But she hates that she flinches.

His hand flush on her cheek now.

Welcome home.

Brushes a curl back from her forehead.

His knuckle on her skin.

Her skin against his knuckle.

She knows that touch.

As real as real.

Milgram developed the technology. He was convinced there was a way to make off-body even better.

When you tap in, you're in a computer construct. Could be open to anyone, could be limited access, or could be something private by request. You might go in alone, you might bring a few friends who tap in by your invitation. Medieval feast, a sultan's harem, Old West cathouse, whatever. But everything else besides you in that world, the horses, the harem girls, the frontier whores, the beds, the feast, the clothes, the props, they're all part of the construct. Just the computer filling in the blanks.

Take the farmboys back at the country church. Me, Harrow, Simon, Mark, we're all people, comatose in our beds somewhere. The farmboys were computer code. Just part of the program, like the pews.

So if a farmboy hits me, I feel pain, because I'm a real

person. And if I hit a farmboy, the punch feels plenty real to me, but the farmboy only simulates a pain reaction. It's the computer's best guess at pain.

The best guess, for most people, is convincing enough.

But not for everyone.

Mina spits on her laptop.

Cheap Chinese piece of shit.

Mark's eyes jitterbug under his lids, like they're searching for the exit.

Margo can't tell if he's dreaming or drowning.

I thought you said you piggyback people all the time.

Not all the time. Sometimes.

So what's the problem?

There's no problem.

Margo stubs out her butt.

I'm bringing him up.

Give me a second.

Both bony hands now free of the keyboard, Mina clutches instead at her wild witch's nest of black hair.

Goddammit. Where are you?

I thought he was riding in with her? You know, like a skateboarder grabbing a bus? That's what you said, right?

Yes.

So where is he?

I think he let go of the bus.

There is a certain kind of off-body customer who wants to, say, humiliate someone sexually. Harbors a dark rape fantasy. Fuck you with a knife to your throat, get off on your screams, that kind of shit. Fear and pain as aphrodisiacs. Brands, whips, blades, etcetera. If you can think it, someone's already thought it and done it. And someone else watched it. And someone else heard about it and wanted to go and do likewise.

In fact, one of the whispered selling points of the limno-sphere, at first, was that it would let people like that burn off that sick energy. At first.

Problem is, to that kind of person, the computer's best guess was never quite good enough.

So that was the first thing Milgram figured out.

The other thing he figured out was something no one else had thought of. Or if they'd thought it, they didn't put it into practice. They didn't dare.

He figured out that it makes a difference to have a real person on the other end. A real person reacting to you. Giving you feedback.

Take Mary and Magdalene, the church twins. The heart of Harrow's big demonstration. The first one, Mary, was just the computer's idea of a girl. The computer's idea of a downy cheek. The computer's idea of a blush.

The second one, Magdalene, was a real girl, tapped into a bed somewhere, feeling everything on the other end. Reacting to my touch.

So, too, was my wife. My Stella.

Someone was playing her part.

Feeling my hands on her face somewhere.

Feeling my kiss.

It's the only way to make it feel that real.

So what Milgram figured out was that you can tap people in, doesn't matter who they are, what they look like out here, once they're off-body you can basically pour them into an empty vessel in the construct, use them as you will. And once they're tapped in, they're prisoners. They can't tap out and they can't control or even interact with the construct. They just provide the feedback. The emotional underpinnings to the simulation. Give it that extra juice that only comes from real pleasure. Or real pain.

Bigger market for that second one, it turns out.

That was Milgram's innovation. New wine, old bottles, that sort of thing, except in this case, it's the other way around. Old wine. New bottles.

Bottles made to be broken.

So what you do is, you conjure up a made-to-order night-mare. Then cast these people as unwitting extras.

Or, in some cases, as the star.

Rachel was a star.

Milgram's tour is done. Now we're just waiting.

Milgram tries to grin, winces, bobs on the balls of his feet. Like we're two businessmen at a convention, waiting for an elevator.

I pipe up.

I want to see him.

He should be with us momentarily.

No. I want to see him now. See that he's actually here.

But he's in his bed. He won't want to be disturbed.

Don't worry. I won't wake him up. Scout's honor.

Milgram glances at his farmboys.

All right. Follow me.

Nods his head at Farmboy Number One. The frisky one.

You too.

And he leads us both to the back of the bank.

To the vault.

What do you want from me?

I want you to come home.

Why would I do that?

Because it's where you belong.

They stroll a golden path together through the garden in the courtyard, enfolded in birdsong and blossoms. An impossible breeze, originating nowhere, ripples the emerald grass. Blades sway.

But you hurt me.

I punished you. I'm your father. That's what fathers do. They punish. Because they love you. No matter what you've done.

I thought that was God's job.

Which part?

The punishment. And the love.

Father. God. At some point, Grace, we're really saying the same thing.

They only tapped Rachel out because someone had heard about her.

Requested her.

Her reactions were said to be extraordinarily—what's the word.

Nuanced.

She was suddenly in high demand.

An out-of-state donor wanted a test-drive. Called and talked to Harrow personally. Harrow explained he would arrange to tap in the donor and put Rachel at his disposal.

But the donor wanted to meet her. Just for a moment. Out here.

In the flesh.

Call me old-fashioned, he'd said.

Harrow outlined the risks of bringing someone back. Of bringing her back. If she spoke a word of what she'd seen to anyone.

The donor reminded Harrow that he had been habitually generous to Crystal Corral. Then he offered to up the donation. Treble it. He was one of Harrow's closest associates.

The Deacons' Circle, Harrow called them.

They had a special room, special black paycards, special beds.

Special requests.

So, against his better judgment, Harrow agreed. Arranged the meeting. Set a time. Had Rachel tapped out and sent to the infirmary. Under medication. Under restraints. Under watch.

But the donor's private jet was delayed an hour on the tarmac. Stranded by a sudden thunderstorm.

Just long enough for Rachel to get word out to Grace.

Plane grounded. Donor fuming. Storm pounding.

The bright sky furious.

A violent squall that just seemed to blow up out of nowhere.

Act of God, all the weathermen said.

The vault stands open. The door is three feet thick.

Inside, a high-end bed.

In the bed, a body.

Wears a suit, like he's been dressed for the occasion by an undertaker.

Silky white hair in a halo around his pale skull.

Gauges gauge. Monitors beep. Respirator hisses.

Milgram dismisses the nurse with a nod. She leaves to linger just outside the vault doorway.

We stand around the bed, me, Milgram, and the farmboy.

Three wise men at the manger.

Harrow's body seems deflated. Each breath an awful rasp.

So delicate-looking I feel like he might crumble if you touched him.

He is an old man, after all.

Made older by all his dreaming.

In Chinatown, needles wobble. A steady beep becomes a frantic SOS.

Margo frowns.

I don't like this. We should wake him up.

Mina waves her off.

If you do, she'll be left in there alone.

She's in there alone now. And from what I've heard about her, I get the feeling she can take care of herself.

No. Not in there.

Mark jerks.

We have to wake him.

We can't.

Do it.

I said I can't.

Why not?

I have to find him first.

The three other farmboys slowly drift within spitting distance of the open vault. Just to remind me they're there.

The frisky farmboy stands guard inside the doorway.

Looks impatient for the breaking-things to start.

He shoots a glance at Milgram.

Milgram sends back a tight little smile, like a telegram that reads, You'll get your turn. Stop.

I make small talk.

So where's your friend? The Magician?

Simon? He's in there too.

Where's his bed?

He's in a separate location. Security protocol. Pastor Harrow never goes off-body unescorted.

That's not what we talked about. She wanted to meet with her father alone.

This is just a formality. Don't worry. They'll all be back soon. How close is she? Bodily, I mean?

She's close.

And you have people with her? To bring her here?

Yes. And don't forget the motorman.

No, of course not. You see, Mr Spademan? There are other ways to resolve things that don't involve spilling blood.

Sure. Or, at least not ours. Right?

He squints. Nods. Tries to laugh like he's in on the joke. A reaction he must have seen somewhere and sporadically tries to re-create.

Grace, you remember Simon.

Simon joins them on the golden path.

Hadn't been there a moment before.

Now you don't see him, now you do.

Harrow turns to her and grips her shoulders, like he's sending her off on a dangerous but necessary journey.

I'm so glad to have you back, Grace. But actions have consequences, my love.

Simon slips behind her. Grabs her arms from behind.

Her father consoles her.

Just remember, nothing that happens in here can hurt you. Not really. Not in heaven. No matter how real it may seem.

Harrow seems to pause for a second, as though searching for a thought, the addled mind of an old man, not what it used to be, but that's not it at all, in fact he's only shifting his weight slightly, and curling his gnarled wounded bird of a hand into an even more gnarled fist, which he sends with all his heaven-assisted fury into the soft center of Grace's baby-swollen belly.

She cries out.

A cry that carries across pastures, statues, fountains.

A cry seeded, like a storm cloud, with sobs.

Harrow leans in to whisper. Sweet intimacy in her ear.

Don't worry. He's fine.

Then straightens himself. Laurel wreath askew.

I have a strong feeling it's a he.

Uncurls his hand.

Grace, why did you think you could hide him from me? For whatsoever you have, I gave unto you. And whatsoever I gave, I can take away. So sayeth the Lord.

No Bible verse she ever learned.

He nods to Simon.

Now, I'm going to leave you two alone for awhile.

Her short sobs betray her. She struggles to swallow them.

Dad, wait. Don't. Wait. Dad, don't you remember the story of the Prodigal Daughter? The story you taught me when I was a girl? How she returns home and all is forgiven?

Oh Grace. Of course I do. But you know me. I've always been more of an Old Testament man at heart.

I ask Milgram, because I'm genuinely curious.

You ever go off-body? Visit heaven? That you created?

Me? No. Unlike many people, I still feel that there's value in the physical world. That it is a blessing to have a body. I believe that's as God intended it.

Me too.

To retreat to some dream, it's wickedness. A temptation.

To embrace the spectral world. And the people who flock to it—well, they seek easy escapes. It's a weakness. Pastor Harrow doesn't see it that way, of course. But to me, bodies are glorious. To be alive is glorious. That is the gift from God. To turn your back on that—

Yes, it's true. Bodies are glorious.

I check my watch.

Milgram frowns.

Do you have somewhere to be?

No. Just something to do.

He glances at the farmboy, who takes a half-step toward me.

I ignore him. Stare down Milgram.

I've always had one question about bodies though. A question for God, I guess.

Really? What is that? Perhaps I can help you.

Why exactly did He make them so fragile?

Go easy on her, Simon. She is my daughter, after all.

Simon steps around her, then turns sharply to Harrow, like a soldier about to salute.

Reaches up with both hands and grabs Harrow's face.

Kisses him on the cheek.

Then steps back and snaps his fingers.

Presto.

A silver coin.

A trick.

Simon shows it to Harrow. Then palms it.

Snaps again.

Another coin.

He holds them both out, one in each palm.

Then brings his hands together.

Shakes them. Coins rattle.

Reproduce.

He opens his hands to show Harrow the bounty.

Thirty silver pieces in all.

So here's the thing about a box-cutter blade.

You can take it out of the box-cutter.

The blade itself is very thin, like a razor blade, only longer. And it's flat enough to, say, tape to the inside of your forearm.

Or on your chest, under your shirt, over your heart.

Frisk-proof.

I work on the farmboy first. The frisky one.

Nothing lethal. Just something quick. And distracting.

While he's on his knees trying to keep what's left of his eyes from dribbling out onto the floor, I pull the vault door closed.

It's a heavy fucker. Tug-of-war, and I'm the anchor.

Beat the other farmboys by a half-step.

They pound with their pistols. Gunshots muffled on the other side.

I give the kneeling farmboy a last meaningful slice across the throat, and he slumps like a split bag of garbage, spilling its wet load onto the floor.

Now it's just me and Milgram.

Mina's white bandage throbs in the light of the laptop like a neon cross at night.

She searches.

She searches.

She searches.

She smiles.

Fucking finally.

———

Oaken doors creak and Mark rushes in and up the path like he's late for a party.

A centurion head in each hand. Like luggage.

Chucks the heads in the underbrush.

Okay, first of all? Piggybacking is bullshit. Pardon my language.

Brushes his hands off. Stands shirtless. Golden curls. White raiment swaddling his loins. Gladiator sandals with straps wrapped to the knees.

Simon smiles.

Harrow's face ashen.

Mark looks himself up and down.

What? Too gay?

Rolls his shoulders like he's prepping for a prize fight. Bounces. Flexes his back.

Spreads the I RULE tattoo.

Letters reassemble.

URIEL.

That's better.

Boxes the air. A one-two jab.

Now, if you'll excuse me one moment.

He bends double. Grunts.

Stands erect.

Grunts again.

Fists clenched.

Then roars.

Wings unfurl.

I know what you did.

Milgram stands steady. Still smiling that unconvincing smile.

I am blameless in God's sight. None but He can judge me.

That may well be so.

I step toward him.

He smiles. Sweats.

So what are you going to do?

I think you know.

What? Kill me, and then—live in this vault forever? There are three armed men out there, waiting for you, and what do you have? A razor blade?

It's a box-cutter.

You know you can't get out of here alive, not without me.

I pause.

He eyes me. Spots weakness. Crack of daylight. Heads straight for it.

I'm telling you, you do this, and we both die.

I stroke my chin, then take my chin-stroking hand and grab the back of his head. Yank him toward me.

For the first time, he squeals.

I whisper.

Fair enough. You first.

I work on his throat, nothing fancy. But with gusto.

Like ripping at a Christmas gift you can't wait to get open.

We're alone in the vault so there's no rush.

When I let him go he falls to his knees.

Penitent.

Having seen the light. And the dying of the light.

His windpipe whistling.

Exit music.

He plays himself offstage.

Harrow calls for someone to tap him out.

No one's listening.

Simon stands by, arms crossed, like a guy at a bus stop

waiting for the crosstown express. Waiting for the inevitable to play out.

Mark hovers.

Persephone holds out a knife in a stained leather sheath. Asks her father.

Do you remember this?

Yes. I gave it to you.

That's right. For what purpose?

To protect yourself.

Right again. But from what?

The evils of this world.

Yes.

And they are many, Grace Chastity. They are many. And I did my best to prepare you.

Yes. They are many.

And to protect you. I tried to. And to teach you to protect yourself.

Yes. But I didn't do a very good job of that, did I? Not when it counted.

I only wanted the best for you. When you cried, I comforted you. When you faltered, I picked you up. When you strayed, I corrected your path. That's all.

Yes. And you taught me to protect myself.

I hope so.

And my baby. I have a baby to protect now too.

I can harbor you both.

She slides the knife from the sheath.

No, I think I can do this.

Checks her watch.

I think I've learned all I need to learn.

———

I stand alone in the vault. Me, and two bodies. Three, counting Harrow.

His sandpaper breath.

Still oblivious.

The box-cutter blade is too slow for my purposes.

And, by now, too dull.

I check under the bed. Find a gym bag, tucked out of sight.

As I was told to expect.

To be honest, I'm kind of surprised.

Unzip.

Check the contents.

A handgun. A hammer.

A spike.

A second spike, for the heart, as a failsafe.

All accounted for.

Six-inch railroad spikes. Further sharpened.

One thing left to do.

Check my watch.

Grace Chastity, I raised you from a little girl.

I know. I remember. I was there.

Look around you. I can offer you everything.

All I see here is a frightened old man.

I'm not frightened, Grace Chastity. I am saddened. To see what you have become.

Yes. I'm a little saddened myself.

These cheap theatrics don't suit you, Grace Chastity. And despite what you might think, all of this? It's just for show. You can't hurt me in here, don't you understand that? You cannot hurt me. You foolish, stupid little girl. Anything you do in here has no meaning in the actual world. And when I find you there, I will reap this pain on you a thousandfold.

All right.

You know I can do it, Grace Chastity.

Yes. I do.

Checks her watch.

It's true I can't hurt you in here. Not really.

Watch beeps.

But I can give you something to remember me by.

My watch beeps and I hammer the spike in. It takes fewer blows than I would have thought.

I'd etched a cross in his forehead with the box-cutter beforehand.

As a target.

Then held the spike steady.

Waiting for my cue.

Just two blows. Straight through.

Fragile. Like I said.

In the dream, Harrow gasps, shocked, a sharp intake, less in pain than in simple surprise.

Then he smiles. Even looks a little embarrassed.

The emperor dethroned.

Glances down at his chest, where she's still twisting.

Blood spreading in a swallowing stain.

This is the moment he will live in forever. Looped. Like a record skipping.

His knife.

Her hand.

His heart.

It's an old bank, but the vault was retrofitted more recently, the security precautions updated after an employee got locked in overnight.

I search for the emergency release.

Luckily I knew about all this beforehand.

A little bird told me.

After all, there's really no reason to try and stop people from breaking out of your vault.

I find the lever and pull it, and shove the door open slowly, and since they're expecting a guy frisked clean with nothing but a razor blade, I get off five clean shots before they even return fire.

Guns. They do have their uses sometimes.

Three shots hit, two with authority.

And the last farmboy standing has lousy aim.

Lucky.

When he falls I distribute the last half of the magazine more or less equally between them. For closure.

The nurse has, for some reason, stuck around.

She's paralyzed in a corner until I wave her toward the exit.

Crepe soles soundless on the marble floor. Until she hits the puddle.

Keeps running.

Tracks blood right out onto Wall Street.

I start searching the extra rooms for Simon's bed.

Mark lands lightly, looking slightly disappointed.

You hardly needed me. Of course, there's still him.

Simon, prepping his exit.

I'm sorry, but I really have to run.

Mark steps up.

You and I started a conversation earlier, back at that country church. We should finish it.

Simon straightens.

Happy to.

Persephone grabs Mark's arm.

Don't.

Simon smiles. Looks her over.

Good to see you. You look well.

She wipes her blade on her dress. Bloodies the flowers.

Just tell us which way.

Simon looks to Mark. Back to her. Then points.

She says to Simon:

Okay. Now go. Fast. I mean it.

Then she gestures to Mark.

Follow me.

I find Simon's bed in the old bank manager's office, but no Simon.

Now you see him, now you don't.

Too bad, because I have that second spike.

I do find another room though.

Six beds.

Six old men.

All tapped in. All dreaming.

Arranged in the round.

Deacons' Circle.

She leads Mark to a different doorway, hidden behind creeping ivy.

When they first walk through, they actually do hear harps.

Harps, then the screaming.

The far-off hopeless cries of the long-since damned.

The room is pitch-black, with only flickering flames to light it.

They wait in the doorway, their eyes straining against the dark.

Their pupils dilate, hungry to let the light in.

Then regret it.

For Mark, the only reference is paintings. Blake. Bosch. But alive.

Persephone recalls something different.

A young woman stabbing herself in a hospital bed.

Persephone speaks first.

I'll need something.

Mark hands her the hurlbat.

She hefts it, one-handed.

What about you?

I keep something handy for special occasions.

In his hands, suddenly, a sword aflame.

Uriel.

In the Bible, the flaming sword is mentioned only once. Held in the hands of the angel Uriel who banished Adam and Eve from Eden. Some scholars read the flaming sword as a metaphor for lightning. Mark is somewhat more literal-minded.

Persephone lit white by the heatless fire.

Wait, how come you get the flaming sword?

Don't forget, I taught Sunday school. And I have a good imagination.

She heads right. He heads left.

Cut their way back toward each other, like explorers clearing brush.

I watch the deacons sleeping. Leave them undisturbed.

Head outside to the bank steps.

Greet Wall Street.

Fresh air. Bright sun.

Wolf whistle.

Eight mangy stragglers assemble. Still way too many dreadlocks.

Remind myself to institute a shaved-heads-only policy.

For now, though, let them work off some of the anger that built up back in the park, over a week of siege and beatings.

Resentment toward society and so on.

Pass out six box-cutters.

One per deacon.

Point the way inside.

Outside the barn, crickets chatter.

Inside, a nurse flips through a magazine.

Someone in a bed murmurs. Awakes. Bolts upright.

A scream.

Then another.

The nurse puts down her magazine.

At Paved With Gold, in every bed, someone's gasping.

Awakened.

Eyes blinking like a newborn.

Born again.

35

The city's quiet.

I leave Persephone, Mark, and the Mangy Eight at my place and take my boat across the river. It's the first truly cold day of the season and there's a flake or two in the air, with winter creeping up the river to tap the city on the shoulder. I dock in Tribeca, walk east among the castles, rough cobblestones underfoot. These ones aren't made of gold, just cobble. Brought over in the bellies of empty cargo ships as ballast, then unpacked here and used to pave a new world.

In Chinatown the first of the last remaining shops roll up their iron shutters and open.

I'd helped the Mangy Eight ditch their bloody clothes and took care of the Deacons and the farmboys and Dave the doorman too. Remember, I used to work as a garbageman. I have access to incineration. I'd say ashes to ashes but that never made sense to me. None of us start out as ash.

In any case, those gents are all now traveling the city as weightless tourists, floating bird's-eye over the streets, burnt to soot-flecks and swirling on the fresh gusts heralding winter.

May well land by accident on somebody's outstretched tongue.

Reverse snowflake.

This city does leave a taste in your mouth.

—————

I head into a knock-off emporium on Canal Street and pull out what's left of my nest egg. Thanks to recent developments, my slush fund is all slush, no fund. Still, I have just enough for a Chinatown shopping spree, to outfit my new naked brood back home.

I hand over the last few bills.

Prodo for everyone.

As I'm walking out, my phone rings.

Unknown number.

Though I know.

Hello Simon.

I'd never told anyone about that place, the Social Club in Hoboken, not Mark, not Rick, not anyone, so imagine my surprise that morning when Simon the Magician pulled out the chair opposite mine.

Made me an offer.

Laid his cellphone on the table.

Trust me. She'll pick up.

Hello Simon.

Well, I'd say that went off without a hitch.

Almost. I'd really hoped to find you in that bank. Give you a proper good-bye.

I thought you might. But I had to jet. Some other time, perhaps.

Spit-crackle of a bad connection. I blink first.

You got your money. So what's next?

I wait. Manage the crisis. Then fill the void.

No, I mean what's next for her.

I'll make sure she's taken care of.

And how are you planning to do that?

Well, for starters, I have you.

Whatever arrangement you have with her is between the two of you. But let's be clear. If I ever see you—

Don't worry. I don't intend to be involved. At least not right away.

And I almost hung up then and there. I should have. But it gnawed.

So I said it.

One last thing, Simon.

Yes?

Congratulations.

He laughs. That laugh.

So she told you.

Not until this morning.

Secrets are so hard to keep. It's a wonder they even call them secrets. Though I guess this one would have come out eventually. So to speak. Listen, Spademan—

Good-bye Simon.

He starts to say something else but before I hear it I pull out the SIM card and drop the handset in the sewer.

Hear his laughing voice echoing all the way down as he tumbles to the underworld.

It wasn't Harrow.

It wasn't her boyfriend.

It was Simon.

Simon the Magician.

Head of Security.

Harrow never knew.

———

Harrow would have killed them both if he had, of course. Killed all three of them—man, woman, and child. Probably killed some other people besides, just for being in the same vicinity.

Harrow had appointed Simon to be personally responsible for his eldest daughter's security.

His job was to watch her.

So he watched her.

One day, she watched him back.

It was a short affair with only one lasting consequence.

A secret with an expiry date.

Or, rather, a due date.

She'd caught me on my way out this morning. Everyone else in the house still asleep. Led me by the hand to a bench by the waterfront.

The baby wasn't the reason she ran. I was right about that, she said. She actually thought that maybe she could stay. In her home. With her family. With her father. That somehow he'd understand.

Before she'd thought that.

Before Rachel.

But not after.

She cried as she told me this.

She'd gone to Simon first. Spilled everything. About her father, about the farm, about Rachel. About what they'd done to her. Hoped Simon would help her. Hoped together they could halt it.

Turned out he knew all along.

———

Winter wind in a rush up the Hudson.

Hugged her knees to her belly on the bench.

Watching the water.

A posture of protection.

Belly getting bigger every day.

I'm sorry I lied. I was scared—

It's okay—

—first of you. Then of my father. And I knew I'd need help—

It's okay. He had plenty of sins to atone for.

—to stop him. Once I knew. I had to stop him. I didn't know how.

It's okay.

And then Simon—

Tugged her close.

It's okay.

And when I said it that last time, I think she finally started to believe me.

It all made sense now, of course. Simon's intercession. The Judas betrayal. But when I shook his hand in the Social Club, I didn't know any of this, and I can't change that, or deny it.

It was a deal with the devil and I took it.

Figured that's what passes for hope these days.

But maybe I'm wrong.

I hope I am.

She and I sat for a bit by the river. On the Jersey side.

Witnessed the sun resurrect itself over the Hudson. Rising up from its nightly tomb.

That daily miracle.

The once-mighty skyline cast in shadow as a consequence.

36.

All the cemeteries have long since filled up.

No one gets to be buried anymore.

Government mandate. Last thing we all have in common.

Rich, poor, sleeper, servant, preacher, heretic. Everyone goes in the fire.

Except Harrow.

I'd wanted to take Harrow's body along with the others to the incinerator but Persephone wouldn't allow it.

Turns out Harrow has a family plot in a churchyard in Vermont.

Bought a generation ago, next to nine dead generations before that, long before the Harrow clan pulled up the stakes of their revival tents and headed south to build a crystal church.

Burial plot. The last luxury item on Earth.

The plot of ground he'd bought by plundering people's souls.

Persephone insisted.

Can't say I understood but it wasn't mine to understand.

So we rented a U-Haul van, backed it up to the bank steps, and packed Harrow's long body in a cardboard box. The kind that cheap beds come in. Body-length. Rick had a million of those lying around.

Still, Harrow was tall. His shoes stuck out the end.

We slid him in, closed the van doors, and drove all night to Vermont.

Me, her, Mark.

Her in the back with the box.

Moonlit night. Vermont churchyard.

Once you get out of the city, you can see so many stars.

Nine generations of Harrows lay side by side, under stone markers.

Number Ten in a cardboard box.

Number Eleven stood by the graveside, weeping.

Number Twelve asleep in her womb.

We didn't bother with paperwork. Just showed up with a shovel and a body.

Work in the light of the highbeams.

I dig the hole.

Spadework.

Mark says a prayer.

I wish I could recount it, but I don't remember it exactly.

Something about our souls, in this world and the next.

Then we lift the box together.

Aim for the fresh scar we'd just cut in the earth.

Harrow always said that he hoped to build a heaven.

We send him six feet in the opposite direction.

Acknowledgments

Gratitude: To my agent, David McCormick. To my editor, Zachary Wagman, who indirectly inspired the writing of this novel and who, many years later, directly (and expertly) guided it to completion. To Molly Stern and the staff at Crown. To my early reader and hardboiled advisor, Howard Akler. To Jonathan Bernstein, Chilly Gonzales, David Haydn-Jones, Janet Murphy, Derek McCormack, Jason McBride, Susan Kernohan, David Marchese, Benjamin Stark, and Jonathan Weiss for support and inspiration in all of its guises. To my parents, especially. And to Julia: my first reader, thoughtful editor, biggest advocate, best audience, and truest friend. You've kept all those promises, and then some.